FUN 學美國英語 閱讀寫作 課本

AMERICAN SCHOOL TEXTBOOK

Reading & Writing

GRADE 2

MP3

作者 Christine Dugan / Leslie Huber / Margot Kinberg / Miriam Meyers 譯者 黃詩韻

FUN 學美國英語 閱讀寫作 課本 2
American School Textbook: Reading & Writing

作　　者	Christine Dugan / Leslie Huber / Margot Kinberg / Miriam Meyers
審　　定	Judy Majewski
譯　　者	黃詩韻
編　　輯	呂紹柔

封面設計	郭瀞暄
內文排版	田慧盈／郭瀞暄
製程管理	蔡智堯
出 版 者	寂天文化事業股份有限公司
電　　話	+886-(0)2-2365-9739
傳　　真	+886-(0)2-2365-9835
網　　址	www.icosmos.com.tw
讀者服務	onlineservice@icosmos.com.tw
出版日期	2013 年 7 月 初版一刷　(080101)

郵撥帳號　1998620-0　　寂天文化事業股份有限公司

・劃撥金額 600（含）元以上者，郵資免費。

・訂購金額 600 元以下者，加收 65 元運費。

【若有破損，請寄回更換，謝謝。】

HOW TO USE THIS BOOK

The **Skill Overview** provides background information about the skill focus for the lesson.

The **Lesson Number** and **Reading Skill** are clearly identified.

The **Reading Tip** provides guidance for reading each lesson.

Reading Passage

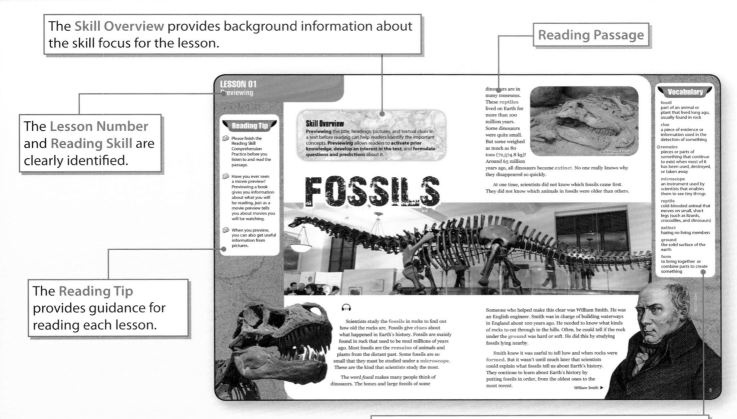

Critical Vocabulary words from the passage are listed.

Power Up summarizes the key terminology and ideas for each lesson.

Comprehension Review helps determine your level of mastery of these strategies and skills.

Word Power reinforces the importance of the critical vocabularies with pictures.

The interactive **Reading Skill Comprehension Practice** helps reinforce the strategy being taught.

Contents Chart

Reading Skill	Subject
Previewing	Social Studies ★ History and Geography
Cause and Effect—Plot	Language and Literature
Headings to Determine Main Ideas	Language and Literature
Main Idea	Social Studies ★ History and Geography
Compare and Contrast	Social Studies ★ History and Geography
Selecting Reading Material	Language and Literature
Character Development	Language and Literature
Topic Sentences to Determine Main Ideas	Social Studies ★ History and Geography
Prior Knowledge	Science
Sequential Order	Social Studies ★ History and Geography
Monitoring Reading Strategies	Science
Problem and Solution—Plot	Language and Literature
Captions to Determine Main Ideas	Social Studies ★ History and Geography
Graphic Features	Science
Chronological Order	Social Studies ★ History and Geography
Structure to Predict	Social Studies ★ History and Geography
Author's Purpose	Science
Chapter Titles to Determine Main Ideas	Visual Arts
Logical Order	Science
Fact and Opinion	Language and Literature
Meaning Clues to Predict	Social Studies ★ History and Geography
Purpose for Reading	Science
Cause and Effect	Social Studies ★ History and Geography
Summary Sentences	Science
Retelling	Language and Literature
Topic to Predict	Social Studies ★ History and Geography
Typeface	Social Studies ★ History and Geography
Proposition and Support	Social Studies ★ History and Geography
Summarizing	Social Studies ★ History and Geography
Questioning	Science

Reading Tip

- Please finish the Reading Skill Comprehension Practice before you listen to and read the passage.

- Have you ever seen a movie preview? Previewing a book gives you information about what you will be reading, just as a movie preview tells you about movies you will be watching.

- When you preview, you can also get useful information from pictures.

Skill Overview

Previewing the title, headings, pictures, and textual clues in a text before reading can help readers identify the important concepts. **Previewing** allows readers to **activate prior knowledge**, **develop an interest in the text**, and **formulate questions and predictions** about it.

FOSSILS

Scientists study the **fossils** in rocks to find out how old the rocks are. Fossils give **clues** about what happened in Earth's history. Fossils are mainly found in rock that used to be mud millions of years ago. Most fossils are the **remains** of animals and plants from the distant past. Some fossils are so small that they must be studied under a **microscope**. These are the kind that scientists study the most.

The word *fossil* makes many people think of dinosaurs. The bones and large fossils of some dinosaurs are in many museums. These **reptiles** lived on Earth for more than 100 million years. Some dinosaurs were quite small. But some weighed as much as 80 tons (72,574.8 kg)! Around 65 million years ago, all dinosaurs became **extinct**. No one really knows why they disappeared so quickly.

A dinosaur fossil

At one time, scientists did not know which fossils came first. They did not know which animals in fossils were older than others.

Someone who helped make this clear was William Smith. He was an English engineer. Smith was in charge of building waterways in England about 100 years ago. He needed to know what kinds of rocks to cut through in the hills. Often, he could tell if the rock under the **ground** was hard or soft. He did this by studying fossils lying nearby.

Smith knew it was useful to tell how and when rocks were **formed**. But it wasn't until much later that scientists could explain what fossils tell us about Earth's history. They continue to learn about Earth's history by putting fossils in order, from the oldest ones to the most recent.

William Smith ▶

Vocabulary

fossil
part of an animal or plant that lived long ago, usually found in rock

clue
a piece of evidence or information used in the detection of something

✪**remains**
pieces or parts of something that continue to exist when most of it has been used, destroyed, or taken away

microscope
an instrument used by scientists that enables them to see tiny things

reptile
cold-blooded animal that moves on small, short legs (such as lizards, crocodiles, and dinosaurs)

extinct
having no living members

ground
the solid surface of the earth

form
to bring together or combine parts to create something

Reading Skill Comprehension Practice

Text formats include **a list**, **a letter**, and **a blog post**.
The information you usually get from a . . .

LIST
- directions
- things you need

LETTER
- things that happen to the person who writes it
- requests

BLOG POST
- review of a restaurant
- personal opinions

Part 1 Look at the pictures in the passage. Based on the pictures, what do you think this passage will be about?

_____

_____

_____

_____

Part 2 Preview the passage. Tell what you think it will be about.

_____

_____

Part 3 What kind of text is this passage? Is it a list? Does it look like a letter? Please answer the questions below.

1. What kind of text is this passage?

_____

2. What kind of information will you learn from this passage?

_____

Comprehension Review

Fill in the best answer for each question.

_____ ❶ **This is probably a _____**
  Ⓐ letter to the editor.
  Ⓑ diary entry.
  Ⓒ section from a nonfiction book.
  Ⓓ set of instructions.

_____ ❷ **The title tells you this will probably be about _____**
  Ⓐ how to do an experiment.
  Ⓑ pioneer life.
  Ⓒ someone's life.
  Ⓓ fossils.

_____ ❸ **Which topic will probably not be discussed in this passage?**
  Ⓐ how to make fossil jewelry
  Ⓑ what fossils tell us
  Ⓒ what scientists do with fossils
  Ⓓ studying fossils

_____ ❹ **Fossils are found mainly _____**
  Ⓐ by William Smith.
  Ⓑ in rock that used to be mud.
  Ⓒ in England.
  Ⓓ in mud.

_____ ❺ **What is another good title for this passage?**
  Ⓐ Fossils and Dinosaurs: What's the Difference?
  Ⓑ How Old Are Rocks?
  Ⓒ Fossils: Clues to Earth's History
  Ⓓ The Man Who Discovered Fossils

_____ ❻ **Someday, _____**
  Ⓐ there will be fossils from our time.
  Ⓑ all fossils will be destroyed.
  Ⓒ William Smith will discover new fossils.
  Ⓓ fossils will not tell us anything.

Word Power

Choose the English word from the Vocabulary list that correctly matches the definition.

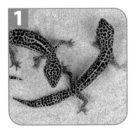 cold-blooded animal that moves on small, short legs (such as lizards, crocodiles, and dinosaurs)

_____

 having no living members

_____

 an instrument used by scientists that enables them to see tiny things

_____

 part of an animal or plant that lived long ago, usually found in rock

_____

Saved by the Bell

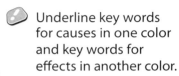
Skill Overview

Cause and effect is a text structure in which the effect happens as a result of the cause. The **cause** is **the event or situation**, and the **effect** is **the consequence of the event or situation**. Knowing the cause-and-effect pattern in texts can help readers better comprehend what they read.

The mice could stand it no longer. From everywhere in the house, they gathered in the Great Hall of Discussion, which was really the old broom closet in the **basement** by the water heater. What was

8

the reason for their meeting? What were they upset about? They needed to decide what to do about their great **enemy**, the cat!

"That cat is so dangerous, she'll **destroy** hundreds of us!" shouted one mouse angrily.

"Thousands!" agreed another.

"Order! Order!" **demanded** a fat mouse with a long tail. He drummed his foot thunderously on the water heater to get everyone's attention.

"Ahem!" he began at last, when all the mice had settled down. From the corner of the basement, a cricket watched with interest. "We are here to discuss what to do about the cat," said the fat mouse.

"She must be stopped!" squeaked a **frightened** voice. It came from a young mouse who had barely escaped the cat's **claws**—claws that were as sharp as fishhooks.

"I agree," said the fat mouse. "We need **protection** from her. But what can we do?"

"I know!" cried one of the mice. She was thin and nervous-looking. She had not dared to steal food from the kitchen for three weeks. "The cat is deadly because we can't hear her coming. We need to be able to hear her, you see?" The mice all nodded in **agreement**.

"But how? What can we do to make the cat louder?" questioned the fat mouse.

"Tie a bell around her!" replied the thin mouse excitedly. "A bell on a collar around her neck—so that every time she tries to sneak up on us, we'll hear the bell!" The mice looked at each other and cheered. This was the best idea anyone ever had for dealing with the cat. A bell! It was perfect! They jumped up and down. The blue flame under the water heater made their shadows as big as kangaroos on the basement wall. The only mouse who wasn't overjoyed was an old mouse who shook his head sadly.

"All right, it's settled," said the fat mouse. "We'll tie a bell around the cat's neck, and we won't need to be afraid of her anymore. Now, who will volunteer to put the bell on the cat?"

Silence. Most of the mice looked down, hoping not to be noticed. Finally, the old mouse spoke up. "Yes, it's easy to talk about an idea, but acting on it is another story!"

Reading Skill Comprehension Practice

Part 1 List **key words** from the story that tell you about **causes and effects**.

finally

Part 2 Fill in the chart below with the correct cause or effect.

Cause	Effect
1. _____	1. The mice had a meeting.
2. The cat was very quiet.	2. _____
3. _____	3. The mice cheered.
4. The fat mouse asked, "Who will volunteer to put the bell on the cat?"	4. _____

Part 3 Please reread the passage and then use your own words to write a sentence about a cause and effect from the passage.

Comprehension Review

Fill in the best answer for each question.

_____ **1** **What caused the cat to be so deadly?**
- Ⓐ The cat stole the mice's food.
- Ⓑ The cat was so quiet that the mice couldn't hear her coming.
- Ⓒ The cat kept stepping on the mice.
- Ⓓ The cat made too much noise.

_____ **2** **What was the effect of the blue flame under the water heater?**
- Ⓐ It made the room too hot.
- Ⓑ It told the mice where the cat was.
- Ⓒ It made the mice's shadows big.
- Ⓓ It had no effect.

_____ **3** **What made the old mouse shake his head sadly?**
- Ⓐ He knew the mice would not put a bell on the cat.
- Ⓑ He was afraid of the other mice.
- Ⓒ He was hungry.
- Ⓓ He was too tired to stay awake.

_____ **4** **Which is an example of a simile*?**
- Ⓐ From the corner of the basement, a cricket watched with interest.
- Ⓑ He drummed his foot thunderously on the water heater.
- Ⓒ The blue flame under the water heater made their shadows as big as kangaroos.
- Ⓓ "Every time she tries to sneak up on us, we'll hear the bell!"

_____ **5** **From whose point of view is the story told?**
- Ⓐ the mice
- Ⓑ the cricket
- Ⓒ the cat
- Ⓓ the bell

_____ **6** **What is the setting of the story?**
- Ⓐ the kitchen
- Ⓑ the basement
- Ⓒ around a campfire
- Ⓓ long ago

* an expression comparing one thing with another, always including the word _as_ or _like_

Word Power

Choose the English word from the Vocabulary list that correctly matches the definition.

 a situation in which everyone agrees about an idea

_____

 to put out of existence; to kill

_____

 a room below the ground

_____

 the act of protecting or state of being protected

_____

Skill Overview

Headings help readers determine the main idea of a text. Headings state a main idea in a word or short phrase and inform readers of what is in the text. Learning to use headings can help increase comprehension.

Oysterville Crate Race

 03

Can You Walk on Water?

Well, maybe you can by stepping on a row of wooden **crates**. The Oysterville Crate Race is a crazy way to take a swim, but a great way to have some fun!

Prizes

- First place in each age group wins $25.
- Runner-up in each age group wins an oyster dinner.

Who Can Enter?

Boys and Girls:

- **Group 1:** ages 10 and under
- **Group 2:** ages 11 and older

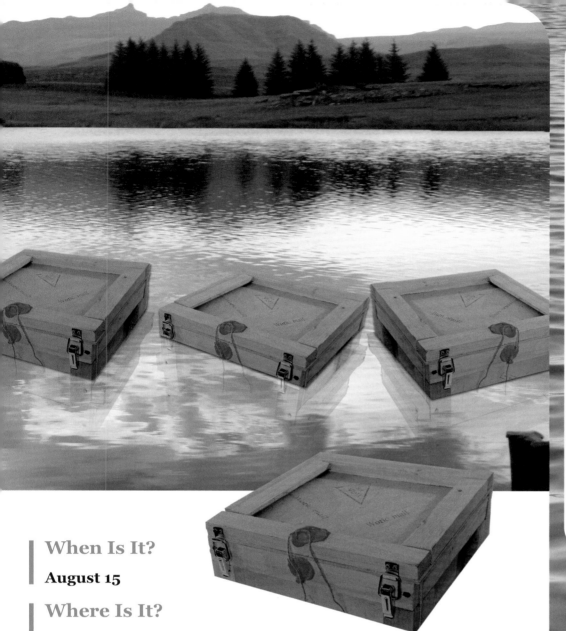

Vocabulary

crate
a wooden box used for carrying things

tie
to fasten together

pier
a walkway over a large body of water

float
to rest or move on or near the surface of a liquid without sinking

balance
to stay in a steady position without falling

object
a goal; an idea

fall off
to become detached and drop

sneakers
light, comfortable shoes that are suitable for playing sports

When Is It?

August 15

Where Is It?

Clear Lake Landing

Rules for the Race

For the race, 50 wooden crates are **tied** together between two **piers**. The crates **float** on top of the water, and racers try to **balance** themselves while they run across the crates as fast as possible. If they make it across all 50 crates, they must turn around and race back across them. The **object** is to cross as many times as possible without **falling off**.

What You Need

- **sneakers**
- a bathing suit
- good balance

13

Part 1 Why did the author choose to include the headings in "Oysterville Crate Race?"

_____

_____

_____

_____

_____

Can You Walk on Water?

Rules for the Race

When Is It?

What You Need

Prizes

Where Is It?

Who Can Enter?

Part 2 Please reread the passage and then use the headings from the text to answer the questions below.

1. When is the Oysterville Crate Race?

_____

2. What three things are needed to compete in this event?

_____

3. What is the first-place prize?

_____

4. What is the rule if you "make it across the crates"?

_____

Part 3 Answer the questions below.

1. What is the main idea of the "Rules for the Race" section?

The main idea is that _____

2. Which section contains the main idea that <u>boys and girls of different ages</u> can enter the contest?

The section is _____

Comprehension Review

Fill in the best answer for each question.

_____ **❶ Under which heading can you find information about what to bring to the race?**
Ⓐ Prizes
Ⓑ Who Can Enter?
Ⓒ When Is It?
Ⓓ What You Need

_____ **❷ Where will you find information about who can race?**
Ⓐ What You Need
Ⓑ Who Can Enter?
Ⓒ Rules for the Race
Ⓓ Where Is It?

_____ **❸ Which information can be found under the heading "Rules for the Race"?**
Ⓐ where the race will be
Ⓑ who may enter the race
Ⓒ what you must do to win the race
Ⓓ what the prizes are

_____ **❹ Why might you read this information?**
Ⓐ to find out when and where something will happen
Ⓑ to find out about Oysterville
Ⓒ to learn about someone's life
Ⓓ to learn how crates are made

_____ **❺ Why do you need a bathing suit to enter the crate race?**
Ⓐ Bathing suits are less expensive than other clothes.
Ⓑ You must swim across the lake to reach the pier.
Ⓒ Bathing suits help you run faster.
Ⓓ The crates float on water, and you might fall into the water.

_____ **❻ A person who likes _____ would probably be interested in this passage.**
Ⓐ cooking
Ⓑ animals
Ⓒ outdoor games
Ⓓ computer games

Word Power

Choose the English word from the Vocabulary list that correctly matches the definition.

 1
a wooden box used for carrying things

_____

 2
a walkway over a large body of water

_____

 3
a goal; an idea

_____

 4
to rest or move on or near the surface of a liquid without sinking

_____

George Washington Carver

Reading Tip

The title of this passage tells you that you will be reading about someone named George Washington Carver. As you read the text, think about what the author wants you to know about Mr. Carver.

Determining the main idea of a passage is one task. It is also important to identify the details that support the main idea.

Skill Overview

The main idea is the overall message of the author. It is the **most important idea** that the author wants to convey or the **central thought** of the passage. The main idea is often expressed directly, or it may be implied. The details are the points that support the main idea.

George Washington Carver never knew his parents. His mother was taken by slave raiders when he was an infant. His father died in a farming accident shortly before his mother was taken. For most of his youth, George was raised by a white couple. They were the Carvers, and they lived in Diamond Grove, Missouri.

▼ The boll weevil had destroyed acres of cotton.

When Carver was 12, he tried to find a school that would allow blacks to attend. His travels took him to Missouri, Iowa, and Kansas. He earned money by working as a farmhand, cook, and laundry helper.

In 1894, Carver graduated with honors from Iowa State College. He took a job there as the director of the **greenhouse**. During this time, he discovered a new kind of **fungus** plant. It grows on the leaves of red and silver maple trees. Many people started to find out about Carver's work in **agriculture**.

Then Tuskegee Institute opened its doors to black students. Carver was asked to head the Department of Agriculture. Not only did he do **research**, but he was also in charge of teaching the farmers. They had been planting cotton for years. But the soil lacked **nutrients**. To make matters worse, the boll weevil had destroyed acres of cotton. Carver told them to plant goobers—what we now know as peanuts—as an alternative **crop**.

That season produced more than enough peanuts. In fact, no one knew what to do with all of them. So, Carver went to work in his lab. He began analyzing the peanut. He found that he could take out a **substance** similar to cow's milk and make cheese from it. After mashing peanuts, he was able to use the oil to make cooking oil, soap, and body oil. And, of course, peanut butter. Overall, he discovered more than 300 **products** that could be made from peanuts.

George Washington Carver died on January 5, 1943. He was buried on the campus of Tuskegee Institute. Five years later, the United States honored him by putting his picture on a three-cent postage stamp.

▲ The stamp with a picture of George Washington Carver

Vocabulary

greenhouse
a building with a roof and sides made of glass

⚙ fungus
a living thing like a plant, but without leaves, that grows where it is wet

agriculture
the practice of growing crops for people to eat

research
the systematic investigation into and study of materials and sources

nutrient
a substance that provides nourishment essential for the maintenance of life and growth

crop
a plant such as a grain, fruit, or vegetable grown in large amounts

substance
any solid or liquid

product
a thing that is the result of an action or process

▼ Carver's peanut lab

Reading Skill Comprehension Practice

 **After you listen to and read the passage, describe the author's main idea.**

1. *I think the main idea of the passage is that George Washington Carver was a great man who deserves our respect.*

2. _____

 **Please think about the main idea you wrote in Part 1 and then reread the passage. Now fill in the supporting details for the main idea you identified.**

Supporting Detail 1

He was raised by a white couple and never had a chance to know his parents.

Supporting Detail 2

He graduated with honors from Iowa State College.

Supporting Detail 3

He dedicated his life to the study of agriculture.

Supporting Detail 4

He died on January 5, 1943, and was honored by people afterwards.

Sketch a **graphic organizer** in the box. Fill it in with details from the passage and from the ideas you wrote about in Parts 1 and 2.

A graphic organizer can be **a chart, a diagram**, etc.

Comprehension Review

Fill in the best answer for each question.

_____ ❶ **Which one would be another good title for this passage?**
- Ⓐ The Story of the Peanut
- Ⓑ The Tuskegee Institute
- Ⓒ The Life of George Washington Carver
- Ⓓ How to Make Cooking Oil

_____ ❷ **This passage is mostly a _____**
- Ⓐ biography of George Washington Carver.
- Ⓑ recipe for making peanut oil.
- Ⓒ history of African Americans.
- Ⓓ time line of the American Revolution.

_____ ❸ **Which sentence tells the main idea of this passage?**
- Ⓐ George Washington Carver lived at the end of the nineteenth century.
- Ⓑ George Washington Carver learned many uses for the peanut.
- Ⓒ George Washington Carver was the son of slaves.
- Ⓓ George Washington Carver was a former slave who became a scientist and an educator.

_____ ❹ **What was one of the primary problems that Carver found with the cotton farmers?**
- Ⓐ There was too much rain.
- Ⓑ The boll weevil had destroyed acres of land.
- Ⓒ The farmers did not know how to grow cotton.
- Ⓓ The farmers had planted too much cotton.

_____ ❺ **What was George Washington Carver's solution to the problem of poor soil?**
- Ⓐ planting peanuts
- Ⓑ adding water to the soil
- Ⓒ growing more cotton
- Ⓓ adding more sand to the soil

_____ ❻ **George Washington Carver probably liked to read books about _____**
- Ⓐ sports.
- Ⓑ science.
- Ⓒ travel.
- Ⓓ Hollywood stars.

Word Power

Choose the English word from the Vocabulary list that correctly matches the definition.

1 a living thing like a plant, but without leaves, that grows where it is wet

_____

2 any solid or liquid

_____

3 the practice of growing crops for people to eat

_____

4 a plant such as a grain, fruit, or vegetable grown in large amounts

_____

A LOOK AT AFRICA

Skill Overview

Authors use a **compare-and-contrast** structural pattern to show similarities and differences between topics, events, or people. Readers may recognize this pattern by the use of certain signal words, such as *like*, *but*, *also*, and *no*.

05

African Grasslands

Tall, thin grasses rustle and sway in the breeze. A herd of zebras runs through the stalks in graceful bounds. In the distance, an elephant's trumpet sounds. This is the world of the grasslands. One of the most beautiful and famous of the grassland areas is the Serengeti Plain. It is found in Tanzania, a country in eastern Africa.

The Serengeti is usually warm and dry. But it does rain from March to May and a little during October and November. In the Serengeti, it is coldest from June to October.

The most important **feature** of grasslands is that they are covered with grass all year long. Grasslands also have trees and bushes, but they are **scattered** and spread apart. Types of trees that grow in the grasslands include palm, pine, and acacia.

The grasses, bushes, and trees are important for animals. Many of them eat these plants for food. Water is also important for all living things. Because of wet and dry seasons and baking from the sun, the soil in some areas of the grasslands hardens. When it rains, the water does not soak into the ground. Instead, it may pool up for many months, providing water for the animals.

acacia

desert pine

Vocabulary

feature
a typical quality or an important part of something

scattered
laid in various random directions

✪ **sand dune**
a hill or ridge of sand formed by strong winds

ridge
a long, narrow hilltop, mountain range, or watershed

annual
yearly; for a year

region
a particular area or part of the world

climate
a type of weather that a place has (e.g., hot, dry, humid)

record
the best performance or most remarkable event of its kind

The Sahara

The Sahara is the largest hot desert in the world. It covers most of North Africa. More than 25 percent of the Sahara is covered by sheets of sand and **sand dunes**. The rest is made up of mountains, stony steppes, and oases. Sand dunes are hills or ridges of sand piled up by the wind. Some sand dunes and **ridges** get to be 500 to 1,000 feet (152.5 to 304.8 m) high!

The Sahara is very dry, but there is an **annual** rainfall in most **regions**. Half of the Sahara receives less than an inch (2.5 cm) of rain a year. The rest of it receives up to 3.9 inches (9.9 cm) a year. The northern and southern parts of the Sahara have slightly different **climates**. But summers are hot all over the desert. The highest temperature ever **recorded** was 136°F (57.7°C) in Libya.

Animal life in the Sahara mainly includes gazelles, antelopes, jackals, foxes, badgers, and hyenas. Plant life includes grasses, shrubs, and trees in the highlands and in the oases along the riverbeds.

antelope

fox

badger

hyena

jackal

gazelle

21

 Signal words for compare-and-contrast patterns:

- like
- unlike
- much like
- as well as
- same
- similar to
- different from
- differs
- while
- however
- yet
- but
- rather
- most

Part 1 Think about the similarities and differences between the African grasslands and the Sahara. Fill in the Venn diagram below.

African Grasslands
Difference

Similarity

The Sahara
Difference

Part 2 Follow the instructions below.

1. What is the difference between the **geography** of the African grasslands and the Sahara?

_____

2. What is the name of the **most well-known grassland area** in Africa? _____

3. List **one reason** you might want to visit either of the places described in the passage.

_____

Part 3 You have learned that signal words can help you identify a compare-and-contrast relationship. Reread the passage and rewrite two sentences from the text using signal words.

1. _____

2. _____

Comprehension Review

Fill in the best answer for each question.

_____ **❶ The African grasslands and the Sahara are both usually _____**
- Ⓐ full of sand dunes.
- Ⓑ covered by grass.
- Ⓒ rainy.
- Ⓓ dry.

_____ **❷ Unlike the Sahara, the grasslands _____**
- Ⓐ are covered with grass all year long.
- Ⓑ get rain all year long.
- Ⓒ have oases along riverbeds.
- Ⓓ have only pine trees.

_____ **❸ Animals more common to the grasslands than the Sahara are _____**
- Ⓐ gazelles and badgers.
- Ⓑ foxes and antelopes.
- Ⓒ zebras and elephants.
- Ⓓ zebras and hyenas.

_____ **❹ The author probably wrote this _____**
- Ⓐ to tell about the history of Africa.
- Ⓑ to tell about different parts of Africa.
- Ⓒ to tell a story about Africa.
- Ⓓ to get you to visit Africa.

_____ **❺ About how much of the Sahara is covered by sand?**
- Ⓐ 39 percent
- Ⓑ 15 percent
- Ⓒ 58 percent
- Ⓓ 25 percent

_____ **❻ If you have forgotten when it rains in the Serengeti, what could you do?**
- Ⓐ Write the words.
- Ⓑ Look at the title.
- Ⓒ Reread the second paragraph.
- Ⓓ Read about annual rainfall.

Word Power

Choose the English word from the Vocabulary list that correctly matches the definition.

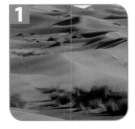
1 a hill or ridge of sand formed by strong winds

_____

2 the type of weather that a place has

_____

3 yearly; for a year

_____

4 a typical quality or an important part of something

_____

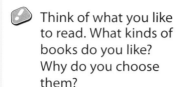

Reading Tip

📎 Think of what you like to read. What kinds of books do you like? Why do you choose them?

📎 There are different ways to select reading material: *recommendation of others, personal interest, knowledge of authors,* and *text difficulty.*

Skill Overview

Selecting reading material is an important skill for readers to have. Readers have different reading levels and interests. By learning how to self-select books, readers will be motivated to read and have a clearer understanding of themselves as readers.

The Lion and the Mouse

From Aesop's Fables, by Aesop

🎧06

Once, when a lion was asleep, a little mouse began running up and down the lion's back. This soon caused the lion to wake up. He then placed his huge **paw** upon the mouse and opened his big **jaws** to swallow him. "Pardon, O King," cried the little mouse. "Forgive me this time—I shall never forget your **mercy**. Who knows when I may be able to return the favor?" The lion was tickled at the idea of the little mouse helping a huge lion like him someday. So he lifted up his paw and let him go.

Sometime later, the lion got caught in a **trap**. The hunters who caught the lion desired to take him alive to the king. So they tied him to a tree while they went in search of a wagon to carry him.

Just then, the little mouse happened to pass by. Seeing the sad situation

that the lion was in, the mouse went up to him and **gnawed** through the ropes that **bound** the king of the beasts. "Was I not right?" said the little mouse.

The **moral** of this **fable** is: Little friends may prove to be great friends.

KAREN LOWE

Vocabulary

paw
the foot of an animal that has claws or nails

jaw ......

paw ......

jaw
the lower part of your face that moves when you open your mouth

mercy
willingness to forgive and show kindness

trap
a device or hole for catching animals or people and preventing their escape

gnaw
to chew

bound
tied up

moral
a lesson to be learned from a story or experience

fable
a short story, typically with animals as characters, conveying a moral

Reading Skill Comprehension Practice

Part 1

Write a sentence identifying what kind of story "The Lion and the Mouse" is.

_____

_____

_____

Genres of Books:

- **Fantasy**
  Harry Potter

- **Adventure**
  Lord of the Rings

- **Science Fiction**
  Rise of the Guardians

- **Historical Fiction**
  Memoirs of a Geisha

- **Realistic Fiction**
  Tuesdays with Morrie

- **Sports**
  Jeremy Lin: The Reason for the Linsanity

- **Mystery**
  Sherlock Holmes

- **Myths**
  Helen of Troy

- **Folk Tales**
  Chinese Animal Zodiac

- **Fairy tales**
  Snow White

- **Legends**
  Steve Jobs

Part 2

Tell whether you would recommend this passage to someone else. Explain why or why not.

1. I would definitely recommend this passage to someone who likes to read fables with a moral.

2. _____

_____

Part 3

We often decide to read something because of our hobbies or interests. What are your interests? What books would you recommend to someone who shares same interests with you?

1. I'm interested in _____

2. **Recommended Books:**

_____

Comprehension Review

Fill in the best answer for each question.

_____ ❶ _____ would like to read this passage.
Ⓐ An animal lover
Ⓑ Someone who likes science
Ⓒ An artist
Ⓓ A person who likes gardening

_____ ❷ This would not be a good choice for someone who _____
Ⓐ is interested in friendship.
Ⓑ likes reading about animals.
Ⓒ loves to read about sports.
Ⓓ enjoys reading fiction.

_____ ❸ People who like _____ would want to read this passage.
Ⓐ mysteries
Ⓑ poetry
Ⓒ biographies
Ⓓ fables

_____ ❹ _"I shall never forget your mercy."_ The mouse says this to the lion because_____
Ⓐ he is upset with the lion for catching him.
Ⓑ he is grateful that the lion didn't eat him.
Ⓒ he wants to trick the lion.
Ⓓ he is usually forgetful.

_____ ❺ Why does the lion decide to let the mouse go?
Ⓐ He is amused by the idea that the mouse could return the favor.
Ⓑ He wants to be friends with the mouse.
Ⓒ He is promised a prize for letting the mouse go.
Ⓓ He is annoyed by the mouse.

_____ ❻ How does the mouse help the lion when he is caught by hunters?
Ⓐ He doesn't help the lion.
Ⓑ He distracts the hunters.
Ⓒ He convinces the hunters to let the lion go.
Ⓓ He gnaws through the ropes that bind the lion.

Word Power

Choose the English word from the Vocabulary list that correctly matches the definition.

1 tied up

_____

2 to chew

_____

3 willingness to forgive and show kindness

_____

4 a short story, typically with animals as characters, conveying a moral

_____

The Special Gift

Skill Overview

The main characters are often the focus of a story. Authors develop their characters by describing their actions, thoughts, physical traits, and relationships. Knowing how characters are developed can help readers understand how stories work and what message the author is trying to get across.

ADMIT ONE 1514744

🎧 07

It was Valentine's Day. For the first time, there were two gifts waiting for me on the kitchen counter—one from my mother and one from my father. Instead of being happy, my heart ached.

I had just been to a friend's birthday party, where I watched her **unwrap** a special gift her father had picked up for her. For me, this was unusual. My mother did all of the special occasion shopping. All my dad did was sign his name on the card, or my mother did it for him. When I **confronted** my dad about this after the party, he didn't say a word. He left the room. My mother cast her disapproving shadow across the room and stated, "I'm disappointed in you. We're a family. How could you hurt your father like that?"

It may sound silly, but when I saw my friend open up her present from her father, I wanted that moment. I wanted my father to want that moment.

Vocabulary

unwrap
to remove the paper or other covering from something

confront
to face, meet, or deal with a difficult situation or person

stationery
things such as envelopes and paper you use for writing

✪ **carousel**
a merry-go-round

✪ **handwritten**
written by hand rather than printed by a machine

desperately
extremely or very much

tinny
thin in tone (as in music, voices, or other sounds)

destination
a place that someone is traveling to

My mother's card to me was beautiful, as always. I knew she had looked over every card in the **stationery** store and selected this one just for me. In the envelope were two movie passes—one for her and one for me. Mother was so thoughtful.

As always, I expected my dad's card to be corny—but it wasn't. On the front was a picture of a **carousel**. I sensed my father had thoughtfully chosen this card, because it didn't seem like a regular Valentine card. When I opened it, I knew I was right. There was no machine-scribed message inside. My eyes misted as I read my father's **handwritten** message.

Wrapped in tissue paper was a small tin of sugar-covered lemon drops. They were my dad's favorite, but he used to share them with me. I wondered where he got them. I placed a lemon drop on my tongue and closed my eyes. I **desperately** tried to remember the rides on the carousel with my father, just as he described them in his message.

I went to put the tin and card in my memory box. When I pulled the box out from under my bed, it tipped and a red ticket stub fluttered out. When I held it in my hand, I remembered. I remembered the **tinny** music, the grasp of my five fingers around my father's hand, and the ponies that brought children to their **destination**. I remembered holding so tightly to the ticket, afraid it would blow away in the wind and I'd miss my special time with my dad. I smiled. I knew my father would never have let that happen— not in the past, and not in the present or future.

power up Main Character **vs.** Supporting Character

- The **main character** of a story is the <u>central or primary personal figure</u>. He or she can also be called a **protagonist**.

- <u>Other characters</u> in the story could be called **supporting characters**.

Part 1 In this passage, the narrator is the main character. Write a few words to describe the narrator.

happy

_____   _____   _____   _____

Part 2 List the other characters in the story. Then write a word that describes each character.

Character's Name	Description
1. a friend of the narrator	cheerful
2.	
3.	

Part 3 In many stories, the main character goes through a number of changes. This is called **character development**. Describe two things that caused the narrator to change.

The narrator changed when she . . .

1. _____

2. _____

Comprehension Review

Fill in the best answer for each question.

_____ ❶ Which is a good word to describe the narrator at the beginning of the story?

Ⓐ happy   Ⓒ sad

Ⓑ terrified   Ⓓ nervous

_____ ❷ Why did the narrator's eyes get misty when she opened her dad's card?

Ⓐ It had a picture of a carousel on it.

Ⓑ It had a personal handwritten message inside.

Ⓒ It was the first card he had ever given her.

Ⓓ It was corny and impersonal.

_____ ❸ Which sentence best shows how the narrator feels about her dad at the end of the story?

Ⓐ I wanted my father to want that moment.

Ⓑ I expected my dad's card to be corny.

Ⓒ Instead of being happy, my heart ached.

Ⓓ I smiled. I knew my father would never let that happen.

_____ ❹ What is the second special gift that the narrator gets from her father?

Ⓐ a tin of sugar-covered lemon drops

Ⓑ a carousel figurine

Ⓒ a memory box

Ⓓ movie passes for the two of them

_____ ❺ What is special about the mother's gifts to the narrator?

Ⓐ They are expensive.

Ⓑ They are thoughtful.

Ⓒ They are large.

Ⓓ They are fun.

_____ ❻ What helps the narrator to remember rides on the carousel with her father?

Ⓐ her Valentine's Day card

Ⓑ a small tin of lemon drops

Ⓒ a red ticket stub

Ⓓ her memory box

Word Power

Choose the English word from the Vocabulary list that correctly matches the definition.

 a place that someone is traveling to

_____

 things such as envelopes and paper you use for writing

_____

 thin in tone (as in music, voices, or other sounds)

_____

 to face, meet, or deal with a difficult situation or person

_____

Reading Tip

Please read the first sentence of the passage, and then follow the instructions in Part 1 before you listen to and read the rest of the passage.

Who Was George Washington?

A portrait of George Washington

Skill Overview

A topic sentence is a general statement that expresses the main idea of a paragraph. It is usually the first sentence in a paragraph and is followed by sentences that support it. The topic sentence prepares the reader to understand the rest of the paragraph.

Vocabulary

revolution
an attempt to change the way a country is governed

measure
to discover the exact size or amount of something

George Washington was an important man in American history. He was a hero in the French and Indian War. He led soldiers in the American **Revolution**. Then, Washington became the first president of a new country.

George Washington was born in Westmoreland County, Virginia. His father died when he was 11. So, he moved in with his brother Lawrence. Lawrence owned a large farm in Virginia called Mount Vernon.

At age 16, Washington became a surveyor of land. He helped

▲ George Washington stepped down after eight years as president.

measure and map new towns in western Virginia.

When Lawrence died, Washington **inherited** Mount Vernon. This plantation became his home for many years.

After the Revolutionary War, people knew that Washington was a great **leader**. So, he was **elected** as the first president of the United States.

Washington believed the country had to have a strong government to be powerful. He asked for help as president. He called his assistants *the cabinet*.

Washington became upset with the U.S. **Congress**. He thought that Congress took too long to make laws. He said he would never go to Congress again. Instead, he would just write letters to them. U.S. presidents still write letters to Congress today.

People wanted Washington to be president for a long time. He did not want to be a **dictator**, so he stepped down after eight years.

Washington moved back to Mount Vernon. He was happy to be home with his wife, Martha. One day, Washington was riding his horse. He became sick with chills and a sore throat. He died that night, on December 14, 1799. He is buried at Mount Vernon.

▲ George Washington became the first president of the United States.

33

Part 1 Think about the first sentence of this passage:

> George Washington was an important man in American history.

This sentence presents the main concept or topic that will be covered in the rest of the passage. What information do you expect to read about in this text? Write your ideas below.

1. *I think I will learn about how George Washington dedicated his life to America.*

2. _____

Part 2 Please find two topic sentences in this passage and record them below.

1. *Washington moved back to Mount Vernon.*

2. _____

3. _____

Part 3 Read the paragraph below, which is missing a topic sentence. Write a topic sentence for this paragraph.

During autumn, leaves are changing colors and falling to the ground. When winter comes around, snow blankets the ground, and temperatures drop so that the air feels icy cold. Spring brings new life to our town, and flowers bloom in the sunshine. Finally, during summer, the sun comes out each day, and the heat feels warm on our skin. Which season do you like best?

Topic Sentence: _____

Comprehension Review

Fill in the best answer for each question.

_____ ❶ "*Washington became upset with the U.S. Congress.*"

Which detail tells you more about this topic sentence?

Ⓐ He was happy to be home with his wife, Martha.

Ⓑ He called his assistants *the cabinet*.

Ⓒ His father died when he was 11.

Ⓓ He thought that Congress took too long to make laws.

_____ ❷ **Which one is not a topic sentence?**

Ⓐ George Washington was an important man in American history.

Ⓑ Washington became upset with the U.S. Congress.

Ⓒ He asked for help as president.

Ⓓ At age 16, Washington became a surveyor of land.

_____ ❸ **Which sentence tells the main idea of this passage?**

Ⓐ George Washington was an important man in American history.

Ⓑ Washington became upset with Congress.

Ⓒ At age 16, Washington became a surveyor of land.

Ⓓ Washington moved back to Mount Vernon.

_____ ❹ **The author probably thinks that _____**

Ⓐ Washington was not a good soldier.

Ⓑ Washington wanted to be a dictator.

Ⓒ Washington does not deserve to be remembered.

Ⓓ Washington was a great president.

_____ ❺ **What caused Washington to step down after eight years as president?**

Ⓐ Congress asked him to step down.

Ⓑ He did not want to be a dictator.

Ⓒ His wife, Martha, asked him to step down.

Ⓓ He was tired of being president.

_____ ❻ **Which sentence best summarizes what this passage is about?**

Ⓐ This is about George Washington, who was a surveyor, a war hero, and the first U.S. president.

Ⓑ This is about how George Washington became a surveyor.

Ⓒ This is about how the U.S. Congress makes laws.

Ⓓ This is about how George Washington became president.

Word Power

Choose the English word from the Vocabulary list that correctly matches the definition.

 a leader with absolute power
_____

 to receive as a gift after someone dies
_____

 to choose for a position
_____

 a person in control of a group, country, or situation
_____

35

An Amazing Machine

Skill Overview

Prior knowledge includes information and experiences to which readers have been exposed. Readers comprehend more when they make connections between what they already know and what they are reading.

ILLUSTRATION BY RICK NEASE

Your body is an amazing machine. A machine has many parts that work together to make it run. In much the same way, a human has body systems that work together to keep a person alive. One **system** is not more important than another. All are **necessary** in order for the body to live. Two body systems that work together are the circulatory system and the respiratory system.

The Circulatory System

The circulatory system moves blood throughout the body. Your **cells** need a **constant** supply of fresh blood. Blood has red blood cells, white blood cells, and platelets. The red blood cells carry oxygen from the lungs to the rest of the body. They also bring back carbon dioxide and waste. White blood cells attack germs to keep the body healthy. Platelets stop bleeding by forming clots. Without platelets, you could bleed to death from a small cut!

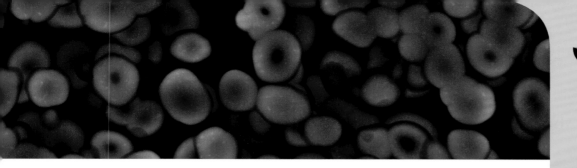

The heart is the pump of the circulatory system. Your heart is about the size of your fist. This muscle pumps blood through blood vessels. Actually, the heart has two pumps. The heart's left pump gets blood from the lungs. This blood has oxygen. The heart pumps it to cells all over the body. The heart's right pump gets the blood returning from the cells. This blood has carbon dioxide in it. The right **pump** moves this blood to the lungs. There, the carbon dioxide is taken out of the blood and oxygen is added.

The Respiratory System

The respiratory system gives the body oxygen and gets rid of carbon dioxide. When you **inhale**, your lungs get bigger, and oxygen rushes into them. When you **exhale**, your chest gets smaller, pushing carbon dioxide out. Air enters through the nose or mouth. Inside your nose are millions of tiny hairs. These hairs trap dust and dirt so that mostly clean air goes down the trachea, or windpipe, to the lungs. Right above the lungs, the windpipe splits into two tubes. One tube enters each lung.

Inside the lungs, these tubes branch into many smaller tubes. These smaller tubes have millions of air sacs. Carbon dioxide and oxygen are **exchanged** in these air sacs. Carbon dioxide leaves the blood and goes into the air sacs. Then oxygen moves through the air sacs into the blood. This oxygen-filled blood goes to the heart. The carbon dioxide leaves the lungs with the next exhale.

ILLUSTRATION BY RICK NEASE

Reading Skill Comprehension Practice

 Fill in the word web with things that you know about <u>the heart</u>.

1. _____

2. _____

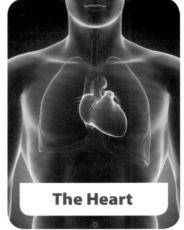

The Heart

3. _____

4. _____

Part 2 Fill in the word web with things that you know about <u>how we breathe</u>.

1. _____

2. _____

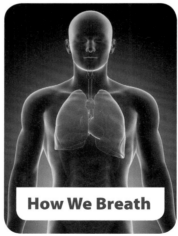

How We Breath

3. _____

4. _____

Part 3 Write two things that you have learned about each system after reading the passage.

1. **Circulatory system:** _____

2. **Respiratory system:** _____

Comprehension Review

Fill in the best answer for each question.

_____ ❶ Knowing what the heart does will help you learn about the _____ system.
- Ⓐ trachea
- Ⓑ circulatory
- Ⓒ respiratory
- Ⓓ carbon dioxide

_____ ❷ If you think about _____, it is easier to learn about platelets.
- Ⓐ air sacs
- Ⓑ carbon dioxide
- Ⓒ lungs
- Ⓓ blood

_____ ❸ You likely know something about _____. This helps you understand how carbon dioxide and oxygen are exchanged.
- Ⓐ the brain
- Ⓑ blood
- Ⓒ breathing
- Ⓓ the stomach

_____ ❹ What do platelets do for your body?
- Ⓐ They form clots that stop bleeding.
- Ⓑ They cause the heart to stop working.
- Ⓒ They help you digest food.
- Ⓓ They make new blood cells.

_____ ❺ To inhale means to _____
- Ⓐ make oxygen.
- Ⓑ breathe out.
- Ⓒ breathe in.
- Ⓓ pump blood.

_____ ❻ You might read this passage if you wanted to _____
- Ⓐ learn how to make something.
- Ⓑ learn about the body's systems.
- Ⓒ read a good mystery.
- Ⓓ read about a famous person.

Word Power

Choose the English word from the Vocabulary list that correctly matches the definition.

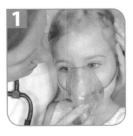 to breathe in

_____

 to trade or give something to someone, who gives you something else back

_____

 to breathe out

_____

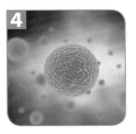 the smallest unit of living matter that can function on its own

_____

Thomas Jefferson

Reading Tip

In this lesson, you will read a short passage about Thomas Jefferson.

Certain words can be a signal to readers that a text has been written in sequential order. These **signal words** include *next, first, last, then, before,* and *later.* Look for these terms as you listen to and read the passage.

▼ Declaration of Independence

Skill Overview

Sequential order is a text structure in which information is presented in an organized way. Incidents, such as historical events, are described in the order in which they occurred. It is best to write about a person's life from beginning to end because a reader can easily follow the order.

A lucky little boy named Thomas Jefferson was born in Virginia on April 13, 1743. Jefferson was lucky because his family lived on a beautiful **plantation** called *Shadwell*. There was lots of land for him to **explore**. He rode horses and learned to hunt. He loved the outdoors.

Jefferson was also lucky because he had an excellent mind. He loved to learn. His family hired **tutors** for him. He read many books each day. He could read in five languages!

Jefferson grew up to be tall and thin. He had red hair and freckles. He was shy and did not talk very much.

When he was almost 17, he went to the College of William and Mary. He was a student there for two years. Jefferson worked very hard. Most days, he studied for 14 hours. He kept notebooks where he wrote down his thoughts about all the things he learned.

Thomas Jefferson's grave site at Monticello in Charlottesville, Virginia.

After college, Jefferson studied **law** for five years. Then he became a lawyer. He traveled all over Virginia. He liked meeting different kinds of people.

Jefferson had many interests besides the law. In fact, it was hard to find a **subject** that did not interest him. He collected books about many different subjects. He especially loved to read about history, science, nature, and **politics**.

Many Virginians were unhappy with their leaders in Great Britain. They did not like being told what to do by a king who lived so far away. Jefferson thought that the people should be able to make their own laws. He wrote about this in booklets and newspaper articles. Later, he became the main author of the **Declaration** of **Independence**. In 1801, he was elected president of the United States.

Jefferson Memorial

Vocabulary

plantation
a large farm on which a particular type of crop is grown

explore
to search and discover

tutor
a person who teaches others, usually individually

law
a rule, usually made by a government

subject
the thing that is being discussed, considered, or studied

politics
the art or science concerned with how governments are run

declaration
an announcement, often written and considered official

independence
freedom from being governed or ruled by another country

41

Compare and Contrast is a structural pattern that shows similarities and differences between topics, events, or people.

Proposition and Support is a text structure in which a problem or idea is presented and then one or more solutions are proposed.

Cause and Effect is a text structure in which effects happen as a result of a specific cause.

Part 1 Tell why you think the author chose to write the passage in sequential order.

Part 2 Make a web of the words and phrases that tell the reader this passage was written in sequential order.

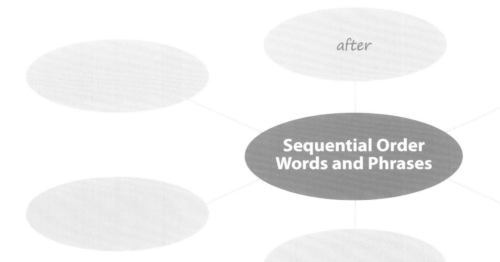

after

Sequential Order Words and Phrases

Part 3 Choose one of the text structures below. Explain how information about Thomas Jefferson might be organized in this new way.

Compare and Contrast

Proposition and Support

Cause and Effect

Comprehension Review

Fill in the best answer for each question.

_____ ❶ **Jefferson studied law before he**
_____

Ⓐ went to the College of William and Mary.

Ⓑ lived at Shadwell.

Ⓒ grew up to be tall and thin.

Ⓓ wrote booklets and newspaper articles.

_____ ❷ **Which did Jefferson do first?**

Ⓐ He went to the College of William and Mary.

Ⓑ He lived at Shadwell.

Ⓒ He studied law for five years.

Ⓓ He traveled all over Virginia.

_____ ❸ **"*Jefferson worked very hard. Most days, he studied for 14 hours.*"**
What happened next?

Ⓐ He went to William and Mary College.

Ⓑ He moved to Shadwell.

Ⓒ He became a lawyer.

Ⓓ He grew up to be tall and thin.

_____ ❹ **Why does the author think that Jefferson was lucky?**

Ⓐ He lived on a beautiful plantation and had an excellent mind.

Ⓑ He grew up to be tall and thin.

Ⓒ He went to William and Mary College and worked very hard.

Ⓓ He collected books about many different subjects.

_____ ❺ **What is a *plantation*?**

Ⓐ a kind of car

Ⓑ a large farm where crops are raised

Ⓒ a very large city

Ⓓ the edge of a river

_____ ❻ **Which does not support the idea that Jefferson had an excellent mind?**

Ⓐ He could read in five languages.

Ⓑ He collected books about many different subjects.

Ⓒ He loved to learn.

Ⓓ He grew up to be tall and thin.

Word Power

Choose the English word from the Vocabulary list that correctly matches the definition.

 a large farm on which a particular type of crop is grown

_____

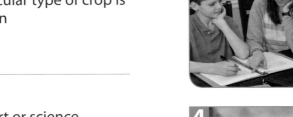 a person who teaches others, usually individually

_____

 the art or science concerned with how governments are run

_____

 freedom from being governed or ruled by another country

_____

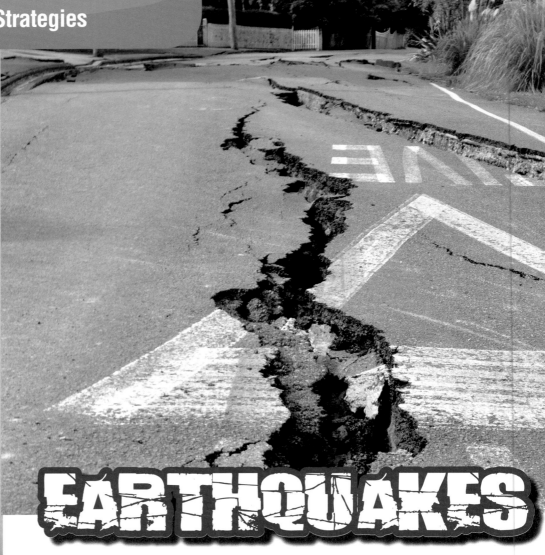

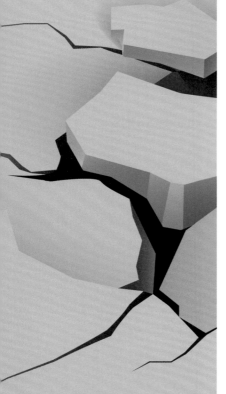

EARTHQUAKES

Skill Overview

Readers who **self-monitor** understand when they are confused by a section of text, when a text does not make sense, and when they are reading too quickly or too slowly. They are then able to modify their reading habits to ensure they understand the text.

When Earth's **crust** moves and the ground shakes, it is called an *earthquake*. It can be caused in many ways: Earth's crust may slide, a volcano may become active, or humans may set off an explosion. Earthquakes that cause the most **damage** result from the crust sliding.

At first, the crust may **bend** because of pushing **forces**. When the pushing becomes too intense, the crust snaps and shifts. Shifting

A fault line

creates waves of **energy** that **extend** in all directions. These are like the ripples you see when a stone is dropped in water. These are called *seismic waves*. The waves travel out from the center of the earthquake. Sometimes people can hear these waves because they make the whole planet ring like a bell. It is both awesome and frightening to hear this sound!

The crust movement can leave a crack, or **fault**, in the land. Geologists—scientists who study Earth's **surface**—say that earthquakes often happen where there are old faults. Wherever there are faults in the crust, it is weaker. This means that earthquakes may happen again and again in that area.

When earthquakes happen under the ocean floor, they sometimes cause huge sea waves. There was an earthquake near Alaska in 1964. Its giant waves caused more damage to some towns than the earthquake did. Some of the waves raced across the ocean in the other direction to the coasts of Japan.

The huge sea waves are called *tsunamis*.

Vocabulary

crust
the outside layer of Earth's surface

damage
harm or injury

bend
to curve

force
physical, especially violent, strength or power

energy
power that is produced

extend
to add to something in order to make it bigger or longer

fault
a crack in the land caused by crust movement

surface
the outer or top part or layer of something

▼ Alaska earthquake in 1964

▼ Seismic waves

TIM BRADLEY

Reading Skill Comprehension Practice

Rereading can help readers remember the passage better.

Making mental pictures or a drawing can help readers understand what they are reading.

Part 1

After listening to and reading the title and the first paragraph, list some of the causes of earthquakes.

Use the rereading strategy if you don't remember the events that can set off an earthquake. After responding, please listen to and read the second paragraph.

1. The earth's crust slides. _____

2. _____

3. _____

Part 2

Once you have listened to and read the second paragraph, think about how Earth's crust splits, causing an earthquake.

Draw a simple picture of **the crust splitting** and then write a short sentence explaining what the picture shows.

_____

_____

Crust splitting

Part 3

After listening to and reading the remaining paragraphs, describe **what an underwater earthquake may cause after it strikes**. Draw a simple picture to match the description.

_____

_____

What an underwater earthquake may cause after it strikes

Comprehension Review

Fill in the best answer for each question.

____ **1** **If you did not remember how an earthquake is caused, what could you do?**

Ⓐ Write the word *earthquake*.

Ⓑ Reread the title.

Ⓒ Read the first paragraph again.

Ⓓ Reread the last sentence.

____ **2** **What is a good way to remember how seismic waves work?**

Ⓐ Write the words *seismic waves*.

Ⓑ Look up the words in a dictionary.

Ⓒ Reread the second paragraph.

Ⓓ Reread the first paragraph.

____ **3** **"Shifting creates waves of energy that extend in all directions...These are called seismic waves."**

If you wanted to learn more about seismic waves, what could you do?

Ⓐ Read the rest of the paragraph.

Ⓑ Look back at the title.

Ⓒ Read the sentences again.

Ⓓ Look up the word *earthquake* in a dictionary.

____ **4** **Which is an opinion?**

Ⓐ The waves travel out from the center of the earthquake.

Ⓑ It is both awesome and frightening to hear this sound!

Ⓒ These are called *seismic waves*.

Ⓓ There was an earthquake in Alaska in 1964.

____ **5** **What is one possible effect of earthquakes?**

Ⓐ a crack that is 3,960 miles long and goes to the center of Earth

Ⓑ volcanic bursts

Ⓒ faults, or cracks, in the ground

Ⓓ a stone dropped in water

____ **6** **What would be another good title for this passage?**

Ⓐ Giant Waves from Nowhere

Ⓑ How Earthquakes Happen

Ⓒ Stay Put When Earthquakes Happen!

Ⓓ Earthquakes in Japan

Word Power

Choose the English word from the Vocabulary list that correctly matches the definition.

 **1** the outside layer of Earth's surface

_____

 **2** a crack in the land caused by crust movement

_____

 **3** power that is produced

_____

 **4** to add to something in order to make it bigger or longer

_____

47

The Secret to Taking Tests

Skill Overview

The elements of story structure are the characters, plot, and setting. The **plot** of a story may include a **main problem** and a **solution**. The problem is a key part of the plot or action of the story.

Kara **struggled** at school. She did things like pressing too hard on her pencil and breaking it or losing her schoolwork. It seemed to Kara that she never did anything right. She **wondered** why she made so many mistakes.

The thing that Kara struggled with the most was her test **scores**. She usually got the lowest score in class, even though she studied hard. One day after school, she told the teacher how she felt. "Look at my math test. I only got 10 right out of 20 problems," Kara said with a look of **disappointment**.

"You just don't know the **secrets** of taking tests," her teacher said.

"There are secrets to taking tests?" asked Kara in surprise.

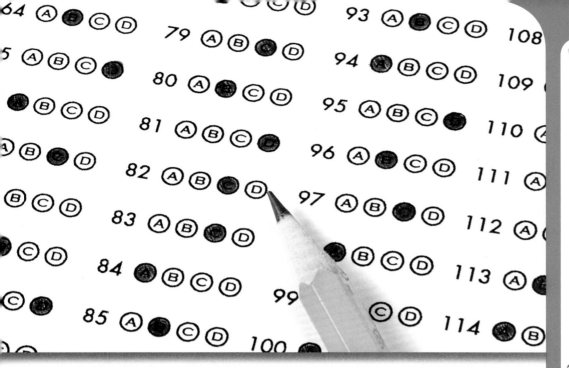

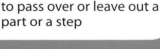

Vocabulary

struggle
to have difficulty with

wonder
to ask yourself questions

score
to win or get a point, goal, etc., in a competition, sport, game, or exam

disappointment
a feeling of sadness because something is not what you expected

secret
a fact about a subject that is not well-known

✪**scoot**
to move swiftly

correct
in agreement with the facts

skip
to pass over or leave out a part or a step

That was the first time she had heard of such a thing.

"Yes, there are, and if you want me to, I will teach them to you." Kara was eager to learn them, so she **scooted** her chair closer to the teacher's desk.

"The first secret to doing well on tests is getting through the whole test. There were 20 problems on your math test. If you worked hard on the first five and got them all **correct**, what are the most points you would score? Yes, five. If you got all the way through 20 problems and even missed 10, what would your score be? Yes, 10. That's twice as many—so it is important to get through the whole test. You do that by following the second secret."

The teacher continued, "The second secret is to do all the easy problems first. You can do this by **skipping** any problems that look difficult. You can also skip problems that you're not sure how to do. In most tests, you have about one minute for each problem, so skip any problems that take more than a minute to do. If you finish the test and there's still time, go back and finish the problems you skipped."

"Are there any more secrets?" asked Kara.

"Yes," said the teacher. "Ask me about them tomorrow, and I will teach the whole class more test-taking secrets."

Kara was excited. She couldn't wait until the next test. She wanted to try out her new secrets because she wanted to see her test scores go up. Maybe the teacher was right—she really could do it!

49

Reading Skill Comprehension Practice

The **Setting** of a story

tells when and where the story takes place. Some stories have specific settings, but other stories take place at an indefinite time or place. Sometimes the setting changes during the story.

The **Plot** of the story

tells what happened. It is the action of the story. It includes a beginning, middle, and end. The plot usually consists of a problem that the main character must solve, the steps the character takes to solve it, the resolution of the problem, and the ending of the story.

Part 1 Reread the passage aloud and answer the following questions about the **characters**.

1. Who is the main character?

2. How does she feel?

3. What makes her feel this way?

4. Who is the other character in the story?

Part 2 Describe the **setting** of the story.

Part 3 Write the **plot** of the story, including the beginning, the middle, and the end.

Beginning

Middle

End

Comprehension Review

Fill in the best answer for each question.

_____ ❶ **This story is mostly about** _____
Ⓐ a person.
Ⓑ a problem and how it is solved.
Ⓒ a time line of events.
Ⓓ how two things are alike and different.

_____ ❷ **In the beginning of the story, you learn** _____
Ⓐ where Kara lives.
Ⓑ how Kara's problem is solved.
Ⓒ who helps to solve Kara's problem.
Ⓓ what Kara's problem is.

_____ ❸ **Where can you find the solution to Kara's problem?**
Ⓐ in the middle and end of the story
Ⓑ in the first sentence of the story
Ⓒ in the beginning of the story
Ⓓ in the pictures

_____ ❹ **When does Kara's point of view about tests change?**
Ⓐ when she asks her parents for help
Ⓑ when she gets 100% on a test
Ⓒ when her teacher gives her test-taking secrets
Ⓓ when she buys a book about taking tests

_____ ❺ **What is the first thing Kara should do when she is taking a test?**
Ⓐ She should do the hardest problems.
Ⓑ She should do the easy problems.
Ⓒ She should do the last problem.
Ⓓ She should do the even-numbered questions.

_____ ❻ **Kara is probably** _____ **that the teacher gave her the secrets to taking tests.**
Ⓐ jealous
Ⓑ angry
Ⓒ scared
Ⓓ grateful

Word Power

Choose the English word from the Vocabulary list that correctly matches the definition.

 a feeling of sadness because something is not what you expected

_____

 to have difficulty with

_____

 to move swiftly

_____

 to ask yourself questions

_____

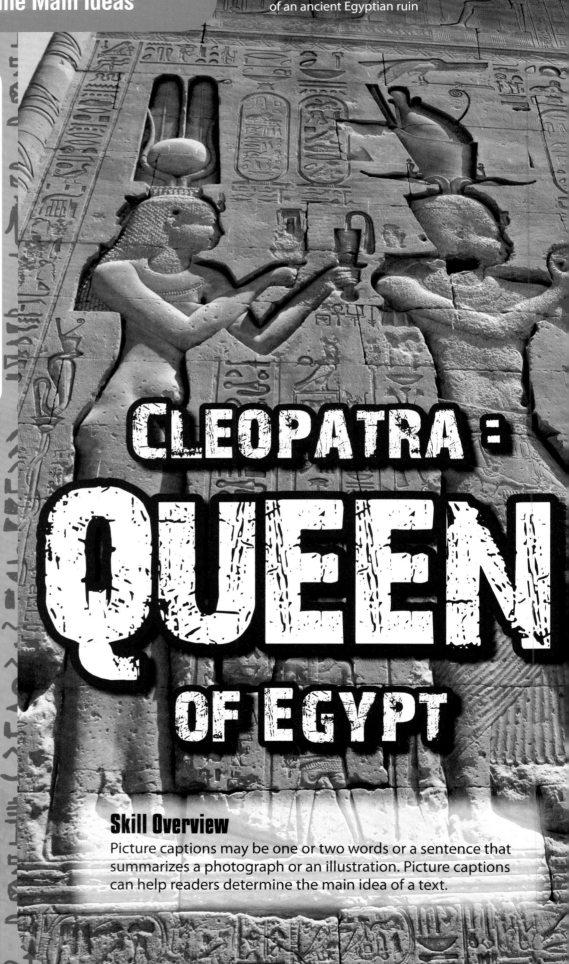

▼ A carving of Cleopatra, Queen of Egypt, on the side of an ancient Egyptian ruin

Reading Tip

Please study the pictures and read the picture captions. Follow the instruction in Part 1 before you listen to and read the passage.

This is a nonfiction passage. This type of passage often includes features that help you better understand the text.

CLEOPATRA :
QUEEN
OF EGYPT

Skill Overview

Picture captions may be one or two words or a sentence that summarizes a photograph or an illustration. Picture captions can help readers determine the main idea of a text.

Cleopatra is one of the most famous women in history. She was beautiful and **ambitious**. Cleopatra lived from 69 to 30 B.C. At the age of 17, she became the queen of Egypt.

While Cleopatra **ruled** Egypt, Julius Caesar was the emperor of Rome. In 48 B.C., he visited Egypt and fell in love with Cleopatra. When Caesar **returned** to Rome, Cleopatra traveled with him. However, Caesar was soon killed. So, Cleopatra went back to Egypt alone.

To **increase** her power, she married a Roman **general** named Mark Antony. Antony was **expected** to become the new emperor of Rome. Soon, he started giving away Roman land to his wife. This angered the Roman general named Octavian, so he **declared** war on Antony and Cleopatra. In a big sea battle, Octavian defeated the Egyptians. Antony killed himself. Cleopatra had lost her power. So, she took her own life as well—by letting a **poisonous** snake bite her.

▲ Mark Antony, a Roman general who married Cleopatra

▼ Roman Emperor Julius Caesar, who fell in love with Cleopatra. He died at the age of 44.

Vocabulary

ambitious
wanting to be successful

rule
to exercise ultimate power or authority over

return
to go back to a previous place

increase
to make something larger in amount or size

general
a high-ranking officer in the military

expect
to think or believe something will happen

declare
to say or state something in an official way

poisonous
very harmful and able to cause illness or death

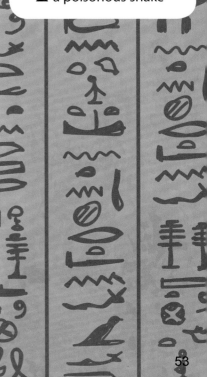

▲ a poisonous snake

Reading Skill Comprehension Practice

Part 1 Write what you learned about Cleopatra by looking at the pictures.

_____

_____

Part 2 Write two things that the picture captions tell you about Cleopatra.

1. _____

_____

2. _____

_____

Part 3

Select a picture caption that describes someone other than Cleopatra.

1. Read the picture caption and write it down.

_____

_____

2. What information does the picture caption provide that cannot be found in the text?

_____

_____

3. Why is it important to read picture captions? _____

_____

Comprehension Review

Fill in the best answer for each question.

_____ **1** **The captions tell you that the statue and carving are of _____**
- Ⓐ Cleopatra and her maid.
- Ⓑ Cleopatra and Marc Antony.
- Ⓒ Julius Caesar and Cleopatra.
- Ⓓ Cleopatra and her daughter.

_____ **2** **The carving of Cleopatra is_____**
- Ⓐ on the side of an Egyptian ruin.
- Ⓑ brand new.
- Ⓒ made of steel.
- Ⓓ too small for most people to see.

_____ **3** **The caption tells you that Julius Caesar was _____**
- Ⓐ Cleopatra's son.
- Ⓑ a Roman emperor.
- Ⓒ the father of Marc Antony.
- Ⓓ bitten by a snake.

_____ **4** **People who like to read about _____ would probably like this passage.**
- Ⓐ dinosaurs and fossils
- Ⓑ outer space
- Ⓒ card tricks
- Ⓓ ancient history

_____ **5** **After Cleopatra went back to Egypt, she _____**
- Ⓐ became queen of Egypt.
- Ⓑ married Julius Caesar.
- Ⓒ married Marc Antony.
- Ⓓ became emperor of Rome.

_____ **6** **Which sentence states the main idea of the passage?**
- Ⓐ Cleopatra is one of the most famous women in history.
- Ⓑ Soon, he started giving away Roman land to his wife.
- Ⓒ When Caesar returned to Rome, Cleopatra traveled with him.
- Ⓓ Octavian defeated the Egyptians.

Word Power

Choose the English word from the Vocabulary list that correctly matches the definition.

1 to say or state something in an official way

_____

2 a high-ranking officer in the military

_____

3 wanting to be successful

_____

4 to make something larger in amount or size

_____

LESSON 14
Graphic Features

Reading Tip

Please look at the pictures in the passage. Then follow the instruction in Part 1 before you listen to and read the passage.

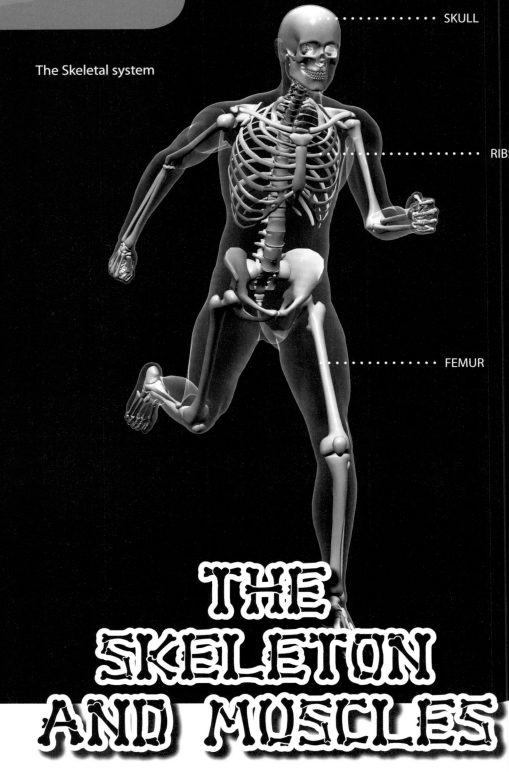

The Skeletal system

SKULL

RIBS

FEMUR

THE SKELETON AND MUSCLES

Skill Overview

Graphic features include visuals—such as **illustration photos**, **diagrams**, **maps**, *tables*, **graphs**, and **charts**—that add meaning to a text. These features help readers get more information from the written page.

Bones are inside every part of your body. Bones **connect** together to make your **skeleton**, and your skeleton gives your size and shape. Each bone in your body has its own important job to do. Some bones, such as your skull, **protect** you. The skull protects your brain. Some bones, such as your ribs, give you shape. Ribs make the shape of your chest and protect your heart, lungs, stomach, and liver. Some bones, such as your femur, or thigh bone, give you **strength** to stand.

Bones may be soft on the inside, but they are hard on the outside. They are made from some of the same things you can find in rocks! These things are called **minerals**. Bones are also dry compared to the rest of the body. A large part of your body is made of water, but only a small part of your skeleton is.

All the bones of your skeleton are connected to each other, except for one. The thyroid bone is in your throat, behind your tongue and above your Adam's apple. **Muscles** hold it there.

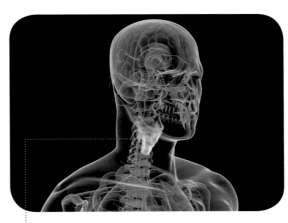

The thyroid bone doesn't connect to other bones.

What exactly are muscles? They are the parts of the body that move bones and make body **organs** such as the heart, lungs, and stomach work. Muscles are also in the walls of blood **vessels** to make blood move.

There are more than 650 different muscles in your body. Your muscles make up a little less than half your total body weight. So, if you weigh 60 pounds, your muscles weigh about 25 pounds.

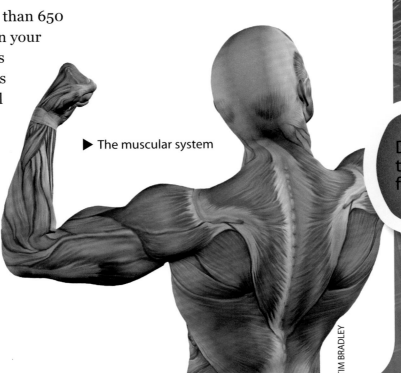

▶ The muscular system

TIM BRADLEY

Vocabulary

connect
to join or be joined with something else

skeleton
the frame of bones supporting a human or animal body

protect
to keep someone or something safe from injury, damage, or loss

strength
the ability to do things that require a lot of physical or mental effort

mineral
natural substance that your body needs in order to stay strong and healthy

muscle
a part of the body that move bones and makes organs work

organ
a part of your body with a specific purpose

vessel
a tube that carries liquids such as blood through the body

Did you know that it takes more muscles to frown than to smile?

Reading Skill Comprehension Practice

Part 1 Write a prediction based on the graphic features in the passage.

1. _I think the passage will introduce the human body._

2. _____

_____

Part 2 Write main ideas about the skeleton and the muscles. Use the graphic features to help you.

Skeleton	Muscles

Part 3 Explain what each graphic feature tells you.

· The graphic of the skeleton tells me . . .
· The graphic of the muscles shows that . . .

_____

_____

_____

_____

Comprehension Review

Fill in the best answer for each question.

_____ **1** What does the picture of the skeletal system show?
- (A) blood
- (B) the heart
- (C) muscles
- (D) bones

_____ **2** What does the picture of the muscular system show?
- (A) leg muscles
- (B) connected muscles
- (C) muscles in blood vessels
- (D) the thyroid bone

_____ **3** Look at the picture of the skeletal system. Which is true?
- (A) The leg bones are the longest bones.
- (B) The skull is the smallest bone.
- (C) The neck bones are longer than the leg bones.
- (D) The rib bones are connected to the leg bones.

_____ **4** Unlike rib bones, your femur _____
- (A) protects your stomach.
- (B) is a bone.
- (C) gives you strength to stand.
- (D) is a muscle.

_____ **5** Which is _not_ something bones do?
- (A) protect
- (B) make body organs work
- (C) determine shape
- (D) give strength

_____ **6** Both bones and muscles _____
- (A) make organs work.
- (B) protect the brain.
- (C) are parts of systems in the body.
- (D) are hard on the outside.

Word Power

Choose the English word from the Vocabulary list that correctly matches the definition.

1  a part of the body that move bones and makes organs work

_____

2 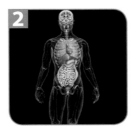 a part of your body with a specific purpose

_____

3  natural substance that your body needs in order to stay strong and healthy

_____

4 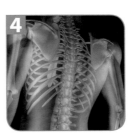 the frame of bones supporting a human or animal body

_____

THE GREEK OLYMPICS

Skill Overview

Authors structure their writing so that readers can understand the information. Text that is written in chronological order tells the time order in which a series of events occurred. Developing an awareness of text structure helps readers understand a text.

 15

In ancient times, athletes arrived in Olympia at least one month prior to the Olympic **competitions**. During this time, they trained physically and were prepared by priests to become pure in thought and deed. Finally, the games would begin.

DAY ONE: The first day of the Olympic Games was spent in religious worship. Each athlete **vowed** to compete with true **sportsmanship**. Animal sacrifices were offered to the god Zeus near his grand temple.

DAY TWO: The second day began with **chariot** races. Races involved two-wheeled carts drawn by four horses. This was followed by an 800-meter bareback horse race. There were also footraces, wrestling, boxing, and horse racing.

DAY THREE: The third day was devoted to the pentathlon, a grueling test of stamina and skill. Contestants competed in five different events in one day—a 200-meter run, wrestling, long jump, discus throw, and javelin toss. All events except for wrestling were held in the **stadium**.

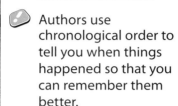
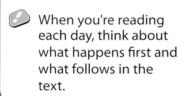

DAY FOUR: The final day of competition started with a 200-meter dash. The rest of the day was devoted to contact sports such as wrestling and boxing. Wrestling contests took place in mud and dust. The dust made it easier to hold onto one's **opponent**; the mud made it more difficult. To win, an athlete had to pin his opponent's shoulders to the ground three times. This method is still used today. In boxing, athletes wore bronze caps to protect their heads from their opponent's fists. Athletes' fists were covered with hard leather that was studded with metal. The final contact event was a combination of wrestling, boxing, and judo. In this event, athletes could punch, kick, and even strangle their opponents until they **surrendered**. To complete the Olympic Games, athletes wearing full armor competed in a 400-meter race.

DAY FIVE: The last day was for celebration. This day usually occurred on a full moon and involved more sacrifices to Zeus. The winners' names would be read aloud before the altar of Zeus. These champions would receive a wreath of olive leaves to wear on their heads. Many won prizes such as olive oil, fine horses, and **privileges** (e.g., not having to pay taxes or being excused from military service). These men returned to their city-states as honored heroes.

Vocabulary

competition
organized event in which athletes or teams compete against each other

vow
to make a determined decision or promise to do something

sportsmanship
the act of showing fairness and respect whether you win or lose

chariot
a two-wheeled vehicle that was used in ancient times for racing and fighting and was pulled by horses

stadium
a large closed area with rows of seats around the sides, used for sports events

opponent
someone you compete against

surrender
to stop fighting and admit defeat

privilege
an advantage that only one person or group of people has

Part 1

Describe what happened on the first day of the Greek Olympics.

1

_____

_____

Part 2

Tell what happened on the remaining days of the Greek Olympics.

Day	Events
2	
3	
4	
5	

Part 3

Number these events in the correct order from 1 to 5.

_____ ○ 400-meter race	_____ ○ chariot races
_____ ○ pentathlon	_____ ○ wrestling and boxing
_____ ○ celebrations	

Comprehension Review

Fill in the best answer for each question.

_____ **1** Which Olympic event happened **first**?
- Ⓐ the pentathlon
- Ⓑ chariot races
- Ⓒ the 200-meter dash
- Ⓓ boxing

_____ **2** Which was the **last** event of Day Four?
- Ⓐ the 200-meter run
- Ⓑ boxing
- Ⓒ wrestling
- Ⓓ the 400-meter race

_____ **3** Athletes competed **after** _____
- Ⓐ they celebrated.
- Ⓑ the full moon.
- Ⓒ they trained physically.
- Ⓓ the second day of the Olympics.

_____ **4** There were five events in the pentathlon. How many sides do you think are on a _pentagram_?
- Ⓐ five
- Ⓑ six
- Ⓒ three
- Ⓓ two

_____ **5** How was wrestling different from the other events in the pentathlon?
- Ⓐ Athletes did not have to train for wrestling.
- Ⓑ It was not a pentathlon event.
- Ⓒ It was not an Olympic event.
- Ⓓ It was not held in the stadium.

_____ **6** What can you guess about Zeus?
- Ⓐ He was an important Greek god.
- Ⓑ He was not important to the Greeks.
- Ⓒ He was a kind of animal.
- Ⓓ He was a Greek slave.

Word Power

Choose the English word from the Vocabulary list that correctly matches the definition.

 a large closed area with rows of seats around the sides, used for sports events

_____

 organized event in which athletes or teams compete against each other

_____

 someone you compete against

_____

 the act of showing fairness and respect whether you win or lose

_____

Niagara Falls: A Changing Natural Wonder

Skill Overview

Text structure provides reader with an understanding of how texts are created. Readers can then use this knowledge to make predictions as they are reading a new text.

Niagara Falls is a beautiful part of the Niagara River. This river is part of what **separates** the United States and Canada. Niagara Falls has two parts: the Horseshoe Falls and the American Falls. Canada owns the U-shaped Horseshoe Falls. The American Falls belongs to the United States. More water goes over Niagara than any other falls in the world. Millions of people visit the Falls each year.

Nature and the Falls

Niagara Falls started out as river **rapids**. Over time, the rushing water wore away the rock of the riverbed. Different kinds of rock **erode** at different rates. Hard dolomite covered soft layers of

Niagara Falls in 1911

Vocabulary

separate
to divide into parts

rapids
a dangerous part of a river that flows very fast because it is steep and sometimes narrow

erode
to slowly wear away

shelf
a long, flat layer of rock that sticks out

gorge
a narrow valley between two hills or mountains

divert
to cause something or someone to change direction

edge
the outer or farthest point of something

······ edge

⭐**unstable**
not safe or reliable

limestone, sandstone, and shale. The rushing water tore away the softer rock. The hard layer was left sticking out like a shelf. Water fell over this **shelf**. The Falls were born!

Twelve thousand years ago, Niagara Falls was seven miles (11.2 km) downstream. Every year, more rock wore away. This made the Falls move back about three feet (0.9 m) each year. Slowly, the Falls moved upstream. This left behind a deep **gorge**

People and the Falls

During the early 1900s, people started **diverting** water from the river above the Falls. This water flows into a power plant and makes electricity. The water is released back into the Niagara River below the Falls. As the demand for electrical power has increased, more water has been taken. Less water going over the Falls means less erosion. Each year, the American Falls moves back about an inch (2.5 cm). Much more water goes over the Horseshoe Falls. It erodes at least 3 inches (7.6 cm) per year.

Horeseshoe Falls

Right below the Falls, the water has worn a hole as deep as the Falls is high! When the lower rock layers wear away enough, the upper ledge will fall. This could be dangerous. Scientists keep track of the Falls' **edges**. They blast away **unstable** edges so that they won't fall when people are standing on them.

American Falls

Reading Skill Comprehension Practice

 **1** What is the main idea of the passage?

_____

Write the important details you learned about Niagara Falls.

Nature and the Falls		People and the Falls

1. _____

_____

2. _____

_____

Niagara
Falls

3. _____

_____

4. _____

_____

Part 2 Write what you might learn if these headings were added to the passage.

Climate	Wildlife	Vacations
_____	_____	_____
_____	_____	_____
_____	_____	_____
_____	_____	_____
_____	_____	_____
_____	_____	_____

Comprehension Review

Fill in the best answer for each question.

_____ **1** This text is a _____.
- Ⓐ letter
- Ⓒ description of a place
- Ⓑ diary
- Ⓓ biography

_____ **2** "*Nature and the Falls*"
What did you read about in this section?
- Ⓐ the number of people who visit Niagara Falls each year
- Ⓑ how nature made Niagara Falls
- Ⓒ where Niagara Falls is located
- Ⓓ how to get to Niagara Falls

_____ **3** "*During the early 1900s, people started diverting water from the river above the Falls.*"
What did you read about *after* this sentence?
- Ⓐ how Niagara Falls was formed
- Ⓑ what kinds of wildlife live at Niagara Falls
- Ⓒ where Niagara Falls is located
- Ⓓ what the diverted water is used for

_____ **4** Which of these is an opinion?
- Ⓐ Niagara Falls is a beautiful part of the Niagara River.
- Ⓑ Millions of people visit the Falls each year.
- Ⓒ During the early 1900s, people started diverting water from the river above the Falls.
- Ⓓ Hard dolomite once covered soft layers of limestone, sandstone, and shale.

_____ **5** Which of these happened *last*?
- Ⓐ Erosion of the Falls decreased.
- Ⓑ River rapids caused erosion.
- Ⓒ A gorge formed.
- Ⓓ The Falls moved upstream.

_____ **6** Why has the rate of erosion changed at the Falls?
- Ⓐ The Falls have reached a layer of very hard rock.
- Ⓑ People have decreased the amount of water that flows over the Falls.
- Ⓒ People have built up the edge with cement.
- Ⓓ People have blasted away unstable edges.

Word Power

Choose the English word from the Vocabulary list that correctly matches the definition.

1 to slowly wear away

_____

2 not safe or reliable

_____

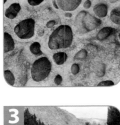
3 a narrow valley between two hills or mountains

_____

4 to divide into parts

_____

MAY THE FORCE BE WITH YOU

Inertia keeps the hockey player gliding across the ice.

Skill Overview

Authors may write for several reasons: to inform, entertain, or persuade. The author's purpose can affect how an author writes, and it is important for readers to recognize this as they read.

🎧 17

A force is anything that pushes or pulls to make an object move. Our world has natural forces. Sir Isaac Newton said that all matter has inertia. Inertia means that any object stays still or moves in the same way until a force acts upon it. For example, a cup placed on a table will stay there until someone or something creates a force to move it. **Inertia** also means that an ice skate will stay gliding across ice in a straight path until the person wearing it changes **direction**, falls, or runs out of ice.

Gravity, which pulls everything toward the ground, is a force. Another is **magnetic** force. Magnets can pull metal objects closer together or push them farther apart.

Friction is an important force, too. Friction works to slow or stop movement between any two surfaces that rub together. Without friction, a person couldn't run. Once that person was moving, he or she couldn't stop. A person couldn't pick up or kick a ball because it would slip away. Hikers wear boots with deep tread to increase friction. Baseball and football players wear cleats for the same reason. A soccer goalie wears gloves to make it easier to catch and hold the ball.

The goalie's gloves apply friction to the ball, and gravity will bring him back down to the ground.

A lack of friction lets things slide. Any smooth surface, such as a kitchen counter, has less friction than a rough surface, such as a brick. Sometimes a lack of friction is good, and other times it's bad. Snow has little friction. This lets skiers glide across it. Cyclists oil the gears on their bikes to make the wheels spin faster. Wet pavement also has little friction. This may cause a car to slide off the road or hit another car.

The swim cap allows the swimmer to glide through the water faster.

Drag is a similar force. Drag is the force of air or water slowing down the things that move through them. Engineers design jets and cars to be **aerodynamic** to **reduce** drag. Then the object slices through the air, letting it move faster. To cut down on the drag in water, swimmers wear caps. This lets them glide through the water more rapidly. Fish have sleek bodies that can move efficiently through water. People design racing boats to do the same thing.

Vocabulary

inertia
property that allows objects to continue moving or remain at rest until a force acts upon them

direction
the position toward which someone or something moves

gravity
the pulling force that keeps things on the ground

magnetic
with the power of a magnet

friction
the force that makes it difficult for one object to slide along the surface of another

drag
the force that slows down as object as it moves through air or water

aerodynamic
made to move easily through air

reduce
to make something smaller in size, amount, degree, importance, etc.

Reading Skill Comprehension Practice

 Authors have a reason for writing. Sometimes that reason is:

to get the reader to believe something or do something.	to teach the reader how to do something.	to share an opinion or a personal experience.

 In the first column below, list the different types of writing you might do. In the second column, describe why you might do that type of writing.

What I Write	Why I Write
1. blog posts	**1.** to record my life
2.	**2.**
3.	**3.**
4.	**4.**

 Explain why you think the author wrote this passage.

_____

_____

 What clues helped you to determine the author's purpose for writing this passage?

Each paragraph has a topic sentence that introduces different force.

_____

Comprehension Review

Fill in the best answer for each question.

❶ Why did the author write this passage?

Ⓐ to explain how forces work

Ⓑ to get you to buy a racing boat

Ⓒ to tell a personal story

Ⓓ to give an opinion about forces

❷ "Cyclists oil the gears on their bikes to make the wheels spin faster."

Why does the author use this example?

Ⓐ to teach you how to ride a bike safely

Ⓑ to describe what a bike is

Ⓒ to show why friction is important

Ⓓ to help explain how friction works

❸ The author hopes that you will _____

Ⓐ learn all about Sir Isaac Newton.

Ⓑ understand how forces work.

Ⓒ buy a pair of skis.

Ⓓ learn to play soccer.

❹ Which athlete performs better when the force of friction is decreased?

Ⓐ a sledder

Ⓑ a soccer player

Ⓒ a mountain climber

Ⓓ a race car driver

❺ Something that is aerodynamic _____

Ⓐ flies high.

Ⓑ cannot crash.

Ⓒ looks modern.

Ⓓ glides through air without difficulty.

❻ Which force pulls things toward the ground?

Ⓐ magnetism

Ⓑ friction

Ⓒ gravity

Ⓓ drag

Word Power

Choose the English word from the Vocabulary list that correctly matches the definition.

1 property that allows objects to continue moving or remain at rest until a force acts upon them

_____

2 made to move easily through air

_____

3 the pulling force that keeps things on the ground

_____

4 the force that makes it difficult for one object to slide along the surface of another

_____

Reading Tip

- Follow the instruction in Part 1 before you listen to and read the passage.

- Chapter titles in both fiction and nonfiction books provide you with information.

- Besides giving you information about the main idea of the chapter, chapter titles also help you **make predictions** and **locate information** easily.

Chapter 5

An Eccentric Artist Diego Rivera

One of Diego Rivera's colorful wall murals

Skill Overview

Chapter titles outline the sequence of a text. They help guide the reader to the categories that frame a book. A chapter is one of the main divisions of a piece of writing. The title of a chapter gives information about the main idea of that chapter.

Part of Diego Rivera's "History of Mexico" mural at the National Palace in Mexico City.

Someone tells you to paint a picture. "All right," you think. "No problem. I can fill the **canvas** pretty easily." But what if the picture you are asked to paint is three stories high, two city blocks long, and one block wide? In other words, a total of 17,000 square feet (1,579 square meters)!

Diego Rivera was one of modern Mexico's most famous painters. When he was asked to paint this huge picture, he did not waver for a minute. In total, Rivera painted 124 **frescos**, which showed Mexican life, history, and social problems.

A fresco is a painting on wet **plaster**. Special watercolors are used. Rivera had to plan ahead and **sketch** what he was going to paint. He used a special plaster. It had to have a certain amount of lime.

Rivera's aides would apply all but the final layer of plaster. Then they used sharp tools to dig the **outlines** of Rivera's sketches into the plaster. Next, they made a mixture of lime and marble dust. This would be spread over the outline in a thin layer. As soon as this layer was firm—but not dry—Rivera would start to paint.

Every morning, his paints had to be freshly mixed. The pigments had to be ground by hand and mixed on a slab of marble. Rivera would not start working until the paints were perfect. Rivera would paint as long as there was daylight. He could not paint under artificial light. It would change how the colors looked.

Some days, he would say that what he had painted that day was not good enough. Then he would **insist** that all the plaster be scraped off so he could start again! It took Rivera years to finish, but this **mural** is thought to be one of the greatest in the world today.

Reading Skill Comprehension Practice

 Use the chapter title **"An Eccentric Artist, Diego Rivera"** to predict what the passage will be about.

I think the passage will be about a unique artist from the past.

_____

 Tell whether your prediction from Part 1 was correct. Then add any new information that you learned to update your prediction.

Yes, my prediction was correct . . .

No, my prediction was wrong. The passage is about . . .

_____

_____

_____

_____

 Chapter titles can help you determine the main idea of a section. Write the main idea of this chapter.

Main idea: _____

_____

_____

Comprehension Review

Fill in the best answer for each question.

_____ ❶ **You will probably not read about _____ in this chapter.**
- Ⓐ Diego Rivera's art
- Ⓑ Diego Rivera's early childhood
- Ⓒ where Diego Rivera lived
- Ⓓ the history of Mexico

_____ ❷ **The title tells you that this passage is mostly about _____**
- Ⓐ traveling in Mexico.
- Ⓑ Mexican food.
- Ⓒ how to paint.
- Ⓓ Diego Rivera's art.

_____ ❸ **The title is a clue that this is a _____**
- Ⓐ recipe.
- Ⓑ letter to the editor.
- Ⓒ biography.
- Ⓓ diary.

_____ ❹ **What was the last thing that happened before Rivera started painting a mural?**
- Ⓐ the outline of the painting was dug into the plaster.
- Ⓑ the thin layer of lime and marble dust was firm.
- Ⓒ he chose the perfect location.
- Ⓓ he made a special plaster.

_____ ❺ **"When he was asked to paint this huge picture, he did not waver for a minute." What is another word for waver?**
- Ⓐ hesitate
- Ⓒ agree
- Ⓑ paint
- Ⓓ run

_____ ❻ **What was the effect of artificial light on the paint?**
- Ⓐ It made the paint dry more quickly.
- Ⓑ It melted the paint.
- Ⓒ It changed how the colors looked.
- Ⓓ It had no effect on the colors.

Word Power

Choose the English word from the Vocabulary list that correctly matches the definition.

 **1** the main shape or edge of something, without any details

_____

 **2** a type of painting done on lime-plaster with water-based paints

_____

 **3** behaving in a way that is different from how most people act

_____

 **4** a large painting done on a wall

_____

Skill Overview

Logical order is a text structure in which ideas are presented in an organized manner. In logical order, ideas are presented in a way that is easy to follow and makes the ideas clear. Logical order includes smooth transitions between ideas.

Nature's Recycling

Stop! Don't throw dead leaves, grass clippings, and fruit and vegetable peels in the trash. Put them to good use in a **compost** pile.

Composting is nature's recycling method. It is a simple way to reuse plant **waste**. Composting breaks down plant materials into **soil** with lots of minerals. Adding composted soil to a garden helps to grow stronger, healthier plants.

Making your own compost is easy. First, gather "food" for **bacteria** and fungi. Then, let them do their job. Just follow these easy steps:

Choose a spot in your yard to place a bin. You can buy one or make one from wire or wood. It doesn't **require** a lid. That way, when it rains, the pile will get wet. Water helps the materials **decay**.

Throw kitchen **scraps** into the pile—things like tea bags, orange rinds, and potato peels. When you cut your grass, add the clippings to the pile. As a general rule, you can add any brown or green plant matter. Although you can put in eggshells, never add animal droppings, cheese, or pieces of meat or fat. These things take a long time to break down.

About twice a month, you must turn the pile to allow the rotting materials to get more air. Use a **shovel** to dig it up a bit. The bacteria and fungi that break down compost need air to live.

Newscom

After just one year, the compost pile will look like soil. This material is called *humus*. Humus contains many other minerals that plants need. Spread the humus on your garden and watch your plants grow. After they die, add them to the compost pile. Then you can recycle those minerals again!

RECYCLE

Reading Skill Comprehension Practice

Part 1 Write three things that need to be written in logical order.

✓ brushing teeth   ✓ putting on clothes   ✓ installing a program

✓ _____   ✓ _____   ✓ _____

Part 2 Imagine you are going to tell someone else how to make a compost pile. Write the steps. Make sure you put them in the right order!

STEP.1

STEP.2

STEP.3

Part 3 Use clue words such as first, then, after, and last to tell how to make a compost pile.

_____

_____

_____

_____

Comprehension Review

Fill in the best answer for each question.

_____ ❶ **What should you do before throwing scraps into a compost pile?**
ⓐ Choose a spot in your yard to place a wooden or wire bin.
ⓑ Turn the pile to allow the rotting materials to get more air.
ⓒ Spread the humus on your garden and watch your plants grow.
ⓓ Add any brown or green plant matter.

_____ ❷ **What is the last step in using compost in your garden?**
ⓐ Choose a spot in your yard to place a wooden or wire bin.
ⓑ Turn the pile to allow the rotting materials to get more air.
ⓒ Spread the humus on your garden and watch your plants grow.
ⓓ Gather "food" for bacteria and fungi.

_____ ❸ **Making a compost heap starts with _____**
ⓐ adding any brown or green plant matter.
ⓑ putting a composting bin in your yard.
ⓒ turning the pile to allow the rotting materials to get more air.
ⓓ spreading the humus on your garden and watching your plants grow.

_____ ❹ **What is the material in a compost pile called?**
ⓐ clay
ⓑ calcium
ⓒ humus
ⓓ phosphorous

_____ ❺ **Why does a compost pile need turning?**
ⓐ so it won't smell so bad
ⓑ so you can reach the humus
ⓒ so it looks better
ⓓ so the rotting material can get more air

_____ ❻ **Which would be good to add to a compost pile?**
ⓐ pieces of fat from a pork chop
ⓑ a banana peel
ⓒ a yogurt cup
ⓓ bits of Swiss cheese

Word Power

Choose the English word from the Vocabulary list that correctly matches the definition.

 small living things that feed on other living things or formerly living things
_____

 to naturally break down
_____

 a pile of leaves, grass, fruits, and other scraps recycled naturally into the earth
_____

 an unnecessary or wrong use of money, substances, time, energy, abilities, etc.
_____

Reading Tip

Both nonfiction and fiction texts may contain facts and opinions. It is important to identify facts and opinions in texts as you read.

You will read a story about two bakers. Try to look for facts and opinions as you read the story.

Skill Overview

A **fact** is something that is true and can be proven with evidence or looked up in an encyclopedia or reference source. An **opinion** is a personal belief or point of view that cannot be verified. It may be an assessment, a judgment, or an evaluation.

The Best Baker in the Land

🎧20

Mrs. Swenson and Mr. Olson each put signs in their bakery windows saying, "The Best Baker in the Land." Back and forth they argued, saying, "I am the best." "No, I am the best." The townspeople soon **wearied** of their **constant bickering**.

Vocabulary

weary
to become tired of or inpatient with

constant
without stopping

✪**bickering**
arguing

royal
having the status of a king or queen or a member of their family

impress
to cause admiration or respect

flour
powder made from grain, especially wheat

yeast
a type of fungus that is used to make bread swell and become light

apron
a protective garment worn over the front of one's clothes and tied at the back

apron

One day, the mayor announced that the king was coming to look for a new **royal** baker. "If one of you wins," he told them, "it will be a great honor."

The two bakers baked for days in order to **impress** the king. When he arrived, he looked over the cakes, cookies, and pies and cried, "But where is the bread?"

The two bakers looked at each other and said, "Bread?"

"You must bake bread for the king!" cried the mayor.

"I have only a little **flour** and milk left," said Mrs. Swenson.

"I only have a little **yeast** and butter," said Mr. Olson.

"Fine. Then together you can bake bread," said the king.

Mr. Olson took his yeast and butter over to Mrs. Swenson's bakery. Mrs. Swenson put on her **apron**, and Mr. Olson put on his hat. The bread was just finished when the mayor ran in yelling, "Hurry! The king is getting impatient." He grabbed the bread from the oven and raced down the street with Mrs. Swenson and Mr. Olson just behind him.

The king tasted the bread and smiled. "This is the best bread I have ever tasted. From now on, you will both be royal bakers and bake my bread together."

Reading Skill Comprehension Practice

 Write one fact and one opinion about each topic.

Topic	Fact	Opinion
School Uniforms		
Pizza		
Video Games		
Basketball		
Homework		

Part 2 Look for facts and opinions in the passage. Record them below.

Fact	Opinion
1. The two bakers baked for days in order to impress the king.	1. This is the best bread I have ever tasted.
2.	2.
3.	3.

Part 3 Read each sentence below. Change each fact into an opinion.

Fact	Opinion
1. The palm tree on the beach swayed in the wind.	
2. The sunset filled the sky with pink and orange streaks.	
3. My grandmother bakes cookies every Sunday.	
4. The driver of the car slammed on her brakes to avoid the cat in the road.	
5. My bike tire is flat because I ran over a nail.	

Comprehension Review

Fill in the best answer for each question.

_____ ❶ **Which one happened first?**
- Ⓐ The king tasted the bread and smiled. "This is the best bread I have ever tasted."
- Ⓑ Mr. Olson took his yeast and butter over to Mrs. Swenson's bakery.
- Ⓒ The two bakers baked for days to impress the king.
- Ⓓ One day, the mayor announced that the king was coming to look for a new royal baker.

_____ ❷ **Which of these is an opinion?**
- Ⓐ One day, the mayor announced that the king was coming to look for a new royal baker.
- Ⓑ Mrs. Swenson put on her apron, and Mr. Olson put on his hat.
- Ⓒ I am the best.
- Ⓓ Mr. Olson took his yeast and butter over to Mrs. Swenson's bakery.

_____ ❸ **Which one tells what the king thought?**
- Ⓐ This is the best bread I have ever tasted.
- Ⓑ The two bakers baked for days to impress the king.
- Ⓒ Mrs. Swenson and Mr. Olson each put signs in the windows of their bakeries.
- Ⓓ One day, the mayor announced that the king was coming to look for a new royal baker.

_____ ❹ **Which one happened first?**
- Ⓐ The king tasted the bread and smiled. "This is the best bread I have ever tasted."
- Ⓑ Mr. Olson took his yeast and butter over to Mrs. Swenson's bakery.
- Ⓒ The two bakers baked for days to impress the king.
- Ⓓ One day, the mayor announced that the king was coming to look for a new royal baker.

_____ ❺ **What problem did Mrs. Swenson and Mr. Olson have?**
- Ⓐ Neither one had to bake bread.
- Ⓑ They each did not have enough ingredients to bake bread.
- Ⓒ They did not know the king wanted to choose a new baker.
- Ⓓ Neither one had money to buy food.

_____ ❻ **At the beginning of the story, Mrs. Swenson and Mr. Olson were _____ of each other.**
- Ⓐ jealous
- Ⓒ glad
- Ⓑ proud
- Ⓓ afraid

Word Power

Choose the English word from the Vocabulary list that correctly matches the definition.

1 arguing

_____

2 without stopping

_____

3 to cause admiration or respect

_____

4 to become tired of or inpatient with

_____

Oscar De La Hoya's 1992 Olympic boxing victory

Oscar De La Hoya

AP PHOTO / MARK DUNCAN / AP

Reading Tip

Oscar De La Hoya competed as a boxer for the United States in the 1992 Olympics. In this lesson, you are asked to read the first paragraph about De La Hoya before making a prediction about the rest of the passage. Please follow the instruction in Part 1 after reading the first paragraph.

Skill Overview

Meaning clues such as titles, pictures, and captions can help readers make predictions about a text. Making predictions helps readers focus as they determine whether their predictions were accurate.

 21

Oscar De La Hoya was walking five blocks from his home when five men with guns jumped out of a truck. They stole his wallet. When Oscar returned home two hours later, he found his wallet there. The robbers must have realized who he was from his ID card and returned it. Who is Oscar De La Hoya?

Oscar was born on February 4, 1973, in East Los Angeles. He lived in a **modest** home with his parents, **siblings**, and grandparents. But there where many problems were he lived: **crime**, drugs, and **gangs**. To keep him safe, Oscar's father took him to a **boxing** gym at the age of six. Oscar was on his way.

In 1992, Oscar flew to Barcelona, Spain. He would compete in the Olympics there. Judging had never been completely fair. It was suspected that some countries were favored over others. But Oscar didn't worry only about beating his opponents—he worried about beating the computer, too.

To try to make judging more fair, a new computer was set up. But the computer system was just as messy and unfair. Each judge was given a keypad with two buttons. Every time a boxer from the red corner scored, the red keypad was pushed. Every time the boxer from the blue corner scored, the blue keypad was pushed. At least three of the five judges had to press the button within one second for a punch to be recorded. What if the boxer scoring the punches had his back to the judge? What if the punch was thrown with such speed that the judge did not see it? What if the judge was cheating or was not pushing the button on purpose? The computer could not answer these questions.

Despite these concerns, Oscar went on to **beat** his opponents and the computer! He was the only American to win a gold medal in boxing in 1992. After his **triumph**, Oscar ran around the **ring** with the flags from the United States and Mexico. He waved the United States flag because he is a U.S. citizen. He waved the Mexican flag to show respect for the country where his parents were born.

Vocabulary

modest
not very big or fancy

siblings
brothers and sisters

crime
illegal activity

gang
a group of criminals who work together

boxing
a sport in which two competitors fight by hitting each other with their hands

beat
to defeat or do better than

triumph
a win or a great success

ring
a special area where people perform or compete

Reading Skill Comprehension Practice

Authors often purposefully place clues in a story to hint at what is to come. This technique is called **foreshadowing**.

 **After reading the first paragraph, write some predictions about the rest of the passage.**

1. *I think the passage will elaborate on who Oscar De La Hoya is.*

2. _____

 **Read your predictions above. Now that you have read the whole passage, think about how accurate your predictions were. Answer the questions below.**

1. Were your predictions correct or not? _____

2. What clues in the text helped you make your predictions? _____

_____

 **Answer the questions below.**

1. Why is predicting an important skill?

_____

2. How can you make smart predictions?

_____

3. Why might you make predictions when you read something in the future?

_____

Comprehension Review

Fill in the best answer for each question.

_____ **1 What can you predict from the title?**
- Ⓐ This passage will be about someone named Oscar De La Hoya.
- Ⓑ This passage will be about how to swim.
- Ⓒ This passage will help me learn to do something.
- Ⓓ This passage will be a letter to the editor.

_____ **2** *"Oscar De La Hoya was walking five blocks from his home when five men with guns jumped out of a truck."*
What happened next?
- Ⓐ The men gave Oscar money.
- Ⓑ The men asked Oscar for directions.
- Ⓒ The men stole something from Oscar.
- Ⓓ The men got out of the truck.

_____ **3** *"In 1992, Oscar flew to Barcelona, Spain. He would compete in the Olympics there."*
This sentence helps you predict that you will read about _____
- Ⓐ the climate of Spain.
- Ⓑ Oscar De La Hoya's family.
- Ⓒ Oscar De La Hoya's childhood.
- Ⓓ the Olympic competition.

_____ **4 Why did the robbers return Oscar's wallet?**
- Ⓐ They wanted him to join them.
- Ⓑ They realized who he was and didn't want to steal from him.
- Ⓒ They didn't find any money in the wallet.
- Ⓓ They realized it wasn't really a wallet.

_____ **5** *"After his triumph, Oscar ran around the ring with the flags from the United States and Mexico."*
What does the word <u>triumph</u> mean?
- Ⓐ failure
- Ⓑ travel
- Ⓒ a great success
- Ⓓ a kind of shoe

_____ **6 Which word describes Oscar De La Hoya?**
- Ⓐ athletic
- Ⓑ lazy
- Ⓒ shy
- Ⓓ unhealthy

Word Power

Choose the English word from the Vocabulary list that correctly matches the definition.

 **1** a win or a great success

_____

 **2** not very big or fancy

_____

 **3** brothers and sisters

_____

 **4** a sport in which two competitors fight by hitting each other with their hands

_____

Reading Tip

People typically read nonfiction texts to get information about a subject. You can read this passage to learn about underwater volcanoes.

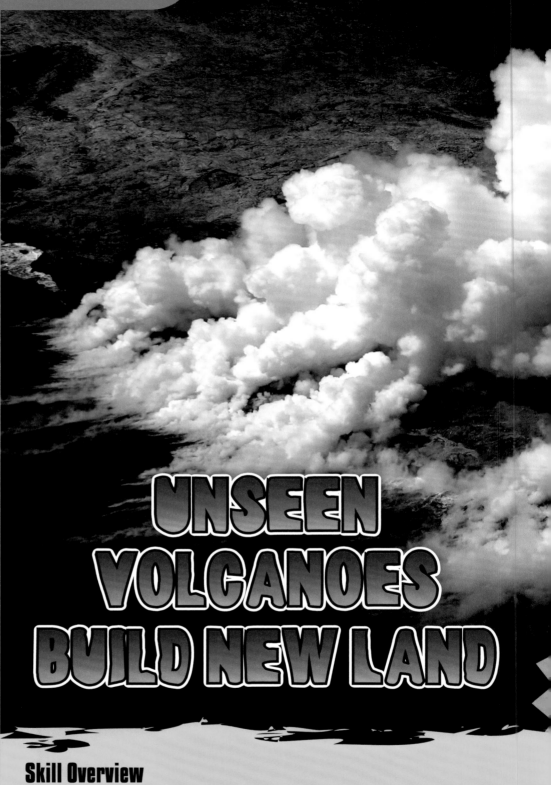

UNSEEN VOLCANOES BUILD NEW LAND

Skill Overview

Readers read for different purposes. They read to understand a specific viewpoint, for information, for fun, or to follow directions. Setting a purpose for reading can help readers better comprehend the material they are viewing.

No one has ever seen some of the biggest volcanoes. Why not? They lie far below the sea!

The biggest mountain **range** zigzags all over the ocean floor. Every day, at least one of its volcanoes **erupts**, causing hot lava to pour out onto the seafloor. The ocean's cold water cools the **lava**, turning it into rock. Layers of this rock build up. If it reaches above the ocean, it forms an island.

Hawaii and Iceland are volcanic islands. Hawaii is growing. Its **active** volcanoes still erupt. Their lava adds more land.

The world's newest volcanic island **appeared** in 1963 near Iceland. Sailors saw a huge cloud of smoke and steam. They sailed closer and saw the birth of a new island. This island kept growing for the next three and a half years.

Even lava that doesn't **reach** above the sea changes land. Over a long time, the lava on the ocean floor **expands** and pushes on the continents. This causes them to move a little bit. Each **continent** moves from one to three inches a year. This means that Earth's surface is always changing. A million years ago, Earth looked different than it does today. A million years from now, it will look different too.

Vocabulary

range
a line of mountains or hills in a row

erupt
to push out smoke, rock, and lava (volcanoes)

lava
hot liquid rock that comes out of the Earth through a volcano

active
erupting often (volcanoes)

appear
to start to be seen or be present

reach
to arrive at a place

expand
to become larger

continent
one of the seven large land masses on the Earth's surface

Seven continents ▲

Hot lava flows across land

The volcanic island Surtsey appeared in 1963.

Cooled lava turns into rock

Reading Skill Comprehension Practice

If we know why we are reading something, it's <u>easier to remember what we read</u> and <u>easier to decide whether a text is a good choice.</u> We read for many different reasons:

- to get information
- to learn how to do something
- for fun

Part 1 Describe something that a person will learn from reading this passage.

_____
_____
_____

Part 2 Would you recommend this passage to someone who wanted to learn about volcanoes? Why or why not?

_____
_____
_____

Part 3 Think about why someone might read the books below. Write a purpose for reading each book based on the title.

Safety Tips for Skateboarding

1. Purpose: _____

_____

The Story of the Pioneers

2. Purpose: _____

_____

Recycle! Don't Waste

3. Purpose: _____

_____

Easy Chocolate Chip Cookies

4. Purpose: _____

_____

Comprehension Review

Fill in the best answer for each question.

_____ **1 You might read this if you wanted to** _____

Ⓐ learn about underwater volcanoes.
Ⓑ make your own volcano.
Ⓒ travel to a volcanic island.
Ⓓ find out what Earth looked like a million years ago.

_____ **2 What could this passage help you do?**

Ⓐ plan a vacation to Hawaii
Ⓑ find a store that sells supplies for making your own volcano
Ⓒ learn how volcanic islands form
Ⓓ find out someone's opinion of volcanoes

_____ **3 You would probably _not_ use this information to** _____

Ⓐ find an example of a volcanic island.
Ⓑ learn how volcanic islands form.
Ⓒ find out where the world's newest volcanic island is.
Ⓓ plan a trip to Iceland.

_____ **4 Which happens _last_?**

Ⓐ A volcano erupts under the sea.
Ⓑ Layers of rock build up, sometimes forming an island.
Ⓒ Lava pours out onto the seafloor.
Ⓓ The lava cools, forming rocks.

_____ **5 How are Hawaii and Iceland similar?**

Ⓐ They both have tropical climates.
Ⓑ They are both in the Atlantic Ocean.
Ⓒ They are both volcanic islands.
Ⓓ They both belong to the United States.

_____ **6 What causes the continents to move a little each year?**

Ⓐ Lava on the ocean floor expands and pushes on the continents.
Ⓑ The continents are pulled toward one another by gravity.
Ⓒ Ocean tides push the continents.
Ⓓ The continents float on the ocean.

Word Power

Choose the English word from the Vocabulary list that correctly matches the definition.

erupting often (volcanoes)

_____

to become larger

_____

to push out smoke, rock, and lava (volcanoes)

_____

to arrive at a place

_____

91

Large king crab

Sea turtle

Trouble in the Coral Reefs

Skill Overview

Cause and effect is a structural pattern that explains an event and the reasons why it happened. Successful readers identify structural patterns and use appropriate strategies to understand the text.

Giant clams

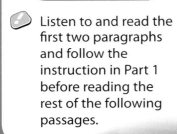

🎧 23

For millions of years, there have been special underwater **ecosystems** called *coral reefs*. They have **provided** homes and food for thousands of living things. Fish and seabirds live near the reefs. They share it with giant clams, sea turtles, crabs, starfish, and many others.

Now, these beautiful places are in danger. So are all the sea plants and animals near them. Scientists blame it on people and **pollution**. We have **ruined** more than one-fourth of Earth's coral reefs. Unless things change, all of the remaining reefs may die soon.

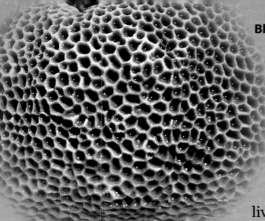

Bleached coral

Vocabulary

⊕ **ecosystem**
a community of organisms and their environments

provide
to supply something that is needed

pollution
things that make the air, water, or soil unclean

ruin
to severely spoil or completely destroy something

rough
not even or smooth

⊕ **polyp**
a small, simple, tube-shaped water animal

⊕ **algae**
simple plants that live in or near water

recover
to get back something lost, especially health

Some people think that coral is stone because it is **rough** and hard, but coral is an animal! Tiny **polyps** form coral reefs. They are many different colors. These colors come from the **algae** living in the coral. The algae are food for the coral polyps.

Billions of coral polyps stick together. New ones grow on the skeletons of dead coral. This happens year after year. Over time, the coral builds up a reef. The reef rises from the ocean floor and grows until it almost reaches the sea's surface.

Coral reefs have been harmed in different ways. People have broken off pieces to sell or keep for themselves. To catch more fish, people have dropped sticks of dynamite into the water. This has blown up parts of reefs. Water pollution has caused the sea plants near coral reefs to grow too much. They block the sun that the algae need.

The worst problem is that the world's oceans are heating up. Warm water kills the algae. When the algae die, the coral loses both its food and its color. The coral turns white and dies. Scientists call this process *coral bleaching*. The bleached part of the coral reef cannot **recover**.

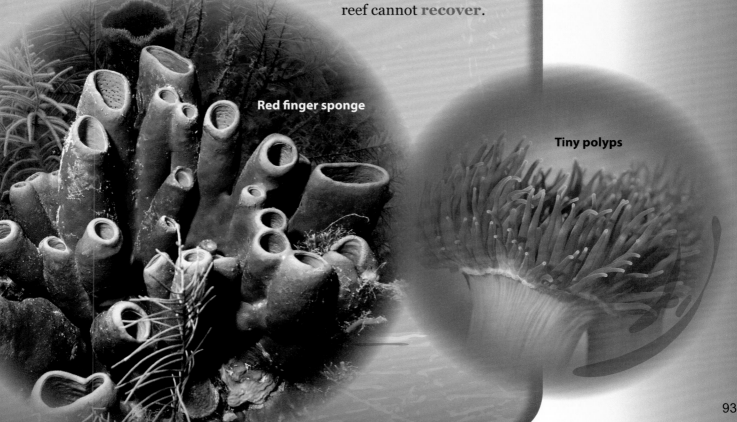

Red finger sponge

Tiny polyps

Reading Skill Comprehension Practice

Part 1 List some things that **cause** harm to coral reefs.

1. _____

2. _____

Part 2 Think about the effects that people and pollution have on coral reefs. Describe these **effects** to someone who may not be aware of the problem.

_____

_____

_____

Part 3 Write the **causes and effects** that you found in the passage.

Cause 1		Effect 1
Warm water kills the algae.	→	When the algae die, the coral loses both its food and color.

Cause 2		Effect 2
_____	→	_____
_____		_____

Cause 3		Effect 3
_____	→	_____
_____		_____

Comprehension Review

Fill in the best answer for each question.

① **Which does *not* cause harm to the coral reefs?**

Ⓐ People break off pieces of coral.

Ⓑ Fish and other wildlife live in the coral reefs.

Ⓒ People blow up coral reefs with dynamite.

Ⓓ The world's oceans are heating up.

② **What is one effect of the oceans heating up?**

Ⓐ Coral reefs have become much larger.

Ⓑ Coral reefs attract more fish.

Ⓒ More coral grows because the water is warmer.

Ⓓ Warm water kills the algae that feed the coral.

③ **What happens when sea plants near the coral reefs grow too much?**

Ⓐ They provide food for more coral reefs.

Ⓑ They cool the ocean.

Ⓒ More fish come to feed on them.

Ⓓ They block the sunlight that algae need.

④ **What are *coral polyps*?**

Ⓐ rocks

Ⓑ plants

Ⓒ animals

Ⓓ algae

⑤ **What is another word for *dynamite*?**

Ⓐ clay

Ⓑ explosives

Ⓒ fire

Ⓓ poison

⑥ **What will probably happen if all of the coral reefs die?**

Ⓐ Many ocean animals will die.

Ⓑ The ocean will get colder.

Ⓒ The ocean will get warmer.

Ⓓ Many sea plants will form reefs.

Word Power

Choose the English word from the Vocabulary list that correctly matches the definition.

 things that make the air, water, or soil unclean

_____

 simple plants that live in or near water

_____

 a community of organisms and their environments

_____

 to severely spoil or completely destroy something

_____

BLIZZARD!

Reading Tip

- Listen to and read the first paragraph, and then follow the instruction in Part 1.

- After responding to Part 1, please listen to and read the following two paragraphs before responding to Part 2.

- Listen to and read the remaining paragraphs after you finish Part 2.

- Paying attention to summary sentences is a good way to make sure you understand the author's main point.

Skill Overview

Summary sentences summarize the information in a paragraph or passage. They help readers determine the main idea. They are usually located at the end of a paragraph or passage. The sentences before the summary sentence give more detailed information.

🎧 24

A **blizzard** is more than just a bad snowstorm. It's a powerful snowstorm with strong, cold winds. Blizzards usually come after a period of warm winter weather. A **mass** of cold air moves down from the Arctic Circle and meets the warmer air. The result is a heavy snowfall **whipped** by bitter north winds. The blowing snow makes it hard to see even a foot or two ahead.

A snowplow removes snow from a city road.

A huge blizzard covered New York City in 1888.

Today, weather reports warn about coming blizzards. But in the past, the dangerous weather came without much **warning**. A huge blizzard in March 1888 covered the eastern United States, choking New York City. It took more than a week to **dig** the city out. During that time, many people froze to death.

Blizzards caused trouble for the settlers in the West, too. People had to **rush** to get themselves and their animals indoors. Otherwise, they would have died. Sometimes people were found frozen just a few feet away from their houses or barns. They just couldn't see well enough to find **shelter**.

It was risky to be out in a storm, yet someone had to feed the animals. So, people **tacked** one end of a rope to their barns. They nailed the other end of the rope to their houses. They went back and forth holding the rope. This kept them from getting lost in the blinding snow.

Blizzards happen in the U.S. Northern Plains states, in eastern and central Canada, and in parts of Russia. The high winds can blow snow into huge drifts 15 feet (5 m) high. These snowdrifts often stop all travel. Schools and businesses close down for days. All the snow must be cleared away. During that time, snowplows may be the only traffic on the roads.

Vocabulary

blizzard
a bad snowstorm with strong, cold winds

mass
a large amount of something

whip
to beat

warning
a sign or signal that something bad is going to happen

dig
to break up and move soil or snow using a tool or a machine

rush
to go or do something very quickly

shelter
protection from bad weather, danger, or attack

tack
to fasten or attach onto something

Reading Skill Comprehension Practice

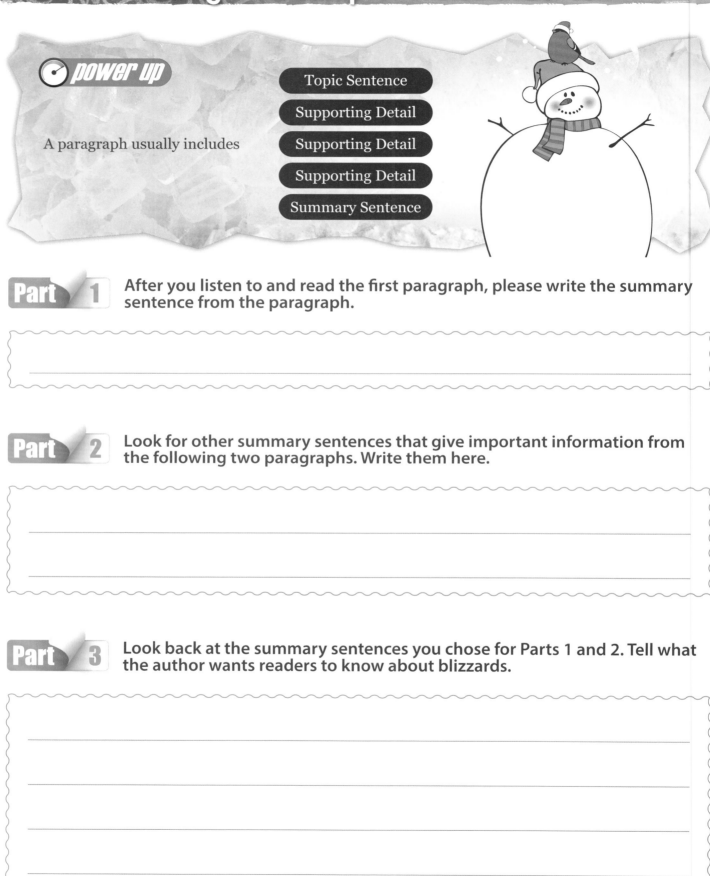

power up

A paragraph usually includes

- Topic Sentence
- Supporting Detail
- Supporting Detail
- Supporting Detail
- Summary Sentence

Part 1 After you listen to and read the first paragraph, please write the summary sentence from the paragraph.

Part 2 Look for other summary sentences that give important information from the following two paragraphs. Write them here.

Part 3 Look back at the summary sentences you chose for Parts 1 and 2. Tell what the author wants readers to know about blizzards.

Comprehension Review

Fill in the best answer for each question.

____ ❶ *"Blizzards caused trouble for the settlers in the West, too."*
Which detail goes with this sentence?
Ⓐ A huge blizzard in March 1888 covered New York City.
Ⓑ A mass of cold air moves down from the Arctic Circle.
Ⓒ People had to rush to get indoors.
Ⓓ Blizzards happen in North America and Russia.

____ ❷ **Which sentence tells the most important idea in the passage?**
Ⓐ A blizzard is a powerful snowstorm with strong, cold winds and heavy snow.
Ⓑ Blizzards can happen in many different places.
Ⓒ A huge blizzard in March 1888 covered New York City.
Ⓓ Blizzards form when a mass of cold air moves down from the Arctic Circle.

____ ❸ **Which one is *not* a good summary sentence?**
Ⓐ A blizzard is more than just a bad snowstorm.
Ⓑ Blizzards caused trouble for the settlers in the West, too.
Ⓒ But in the past, the dangerous weather came without much warning.
Ⓓ This kept them from getting lost in the blinding snow.

____ ❹ **What makes a blizzard unique?**
Ⓐ A blizzard has lots of snow but no wind.
Ⓑ A blizzard has high winds that blow lots of snow around.
Ⓒ A blizzard has high winds but no snow.
Ⓓ No one knows when a blizzard is coming.

____ ❺ **Why does transportation usually halt during a blizzard?**
Ⓐ The rain bury all vehicles.
Ⓑ Winds blow the vehicles off the road.
Ⓒ It's too cold for engines to run.
Ⓓ People can't see well enough to drive or to fly.

____ ❻ **What does *visibility* mean?**
Ⓐ how well you can smell
Ⓑ how well you can see
Ⓒ how well you can hear
Ⓓ how well you can feel

Word Power

Choose the English word from the Vocabulary list that correctly matches the definition.

 protection from bad weather, danger, or attack

_____

 a large amount of something

_____

 a sign or signal that something bad is going to happen

_____

 a bad snowstorm with strong, cold winds

_____

99

I WANT TO BE AN EXPLORER

Skill Overview

Retelling information in a text means to put an author's words into one's own words. This allows readers to repeat ideas in an original way, which helps them to deepen their understanding of what they have read.

🎧 25

I have always wanted to be an **explorer**. Columbus, Magellan, Lewis and Clark, and the astronauts are my heroes. I love reading stories about their **adventures**. It must have been exciting taking off for new places, not knowing what they'd find.

One day in school, we were telling what we wanted to be and do. I said I wanted to be an explorer and find strange and wonderful places. Others laughed and told me there is nowhere left to explore. Even if there was, I am too young to go.

Then my teacher said, "It's not really true that John can't be an explorer or that he is too young. In fact, if he can get someone to take him, he could start exploring strange and interesting places this weekend!"

The class looked **puzzled**. One of the boys asked, "What would he explore? Where would he go?"

A girl said, "He could explore our **garage**. My mother says you could get lost in there with all the **weird** junk." Everyone in the class laughed.

The teacher laughed, too. Then she said, "Exploring your garage might be fun, but there are much better places to go. And they are not that far away."

The teacher took out a paperback book and read the title to the class: *How to Find Unexplored Places Right in Your Own Backyard*. The teacher explained that "in your own backyard" means places close to where you live. She leafed through the book and started reading, "There are ice caves, hot springs, and even an old ghost town near Parkersville."

"That's not far from here!" cried the class.

"Yes. But even if you can't get to Parkersville, you can explore many things right here in our city." She continued reading from the book. It told about the **wonders** of the big central library. It talked about the nooks and crannies in the old train station. And it even mentioned a few museums we'd never heard of. "So you can be an explorer right where you are, even today," she said. "And you are never too old or too young to start."

The class didn't think it was **foolish** to want to be an explorer anymore. In fact, quite a few of them **decided** to become weekend explorers!

Vocabulary

⭐**explorer**
someone who travels to unknown places to find out about them

adventure
an exciting trip or journey

puzzled
confused

garage
a building where a car is kept, built next to or as part of a house

weird
very strange and unusual, unexpected, or not natural

wonder
something that causes a feeling of great surprise and admiration

foolish
unwise, stupid

decide
to choose something

Reading Skill Comprehension Practice

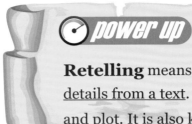

Retelling means <u>to say or write in your own words the main idea and important details from a text</u>. It requires using some details about the main characters, setting, and plot. It is also known as **paraphrasing**.

Part 1 Write three important details from the passage. Tell them in your own words.

1. *The author always wanted to be an explorer like Columbus, Magellan, and Lewis and Clark.*

2. _____

3. _____

4. _____

Part 2 Write a sentence telling the main idea of the passage.

_____

Part 3 Fill in the boxes to map out what happens in the passage.

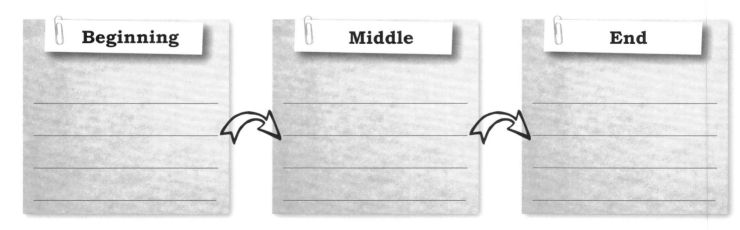

Beginning

Middle

End

Comprehension Review

Fill in the best answer for each question.

_____ ❶ **How might you tell someone else what _in your own backyard_ means?**

Ⓐ It means someplace close to where a person lives.

Ⓑ It means in a person's house.

Ⓒ It means something buried in a garden.

Ⓓ It means a place that a person owns.

_____ ❷ **How did the teacher tell the class about exploring?**

Ⓐ The teacher asked the students what they wanted to study.

Ⓑ The teacher told the class that exploring a garage is fun.

Ⓒ The teacher read to the class about some local places to explore.

Ⓓ The teacher showed the class some pictures.

_____ ❸ **Which one explains why the class laughed at John's wanting to become an explorer?**

Ⓐ The teacher said he was too young.

Ⓑ Someone said he didn't have enough experience for that.

Ⓒ John wanted to be an explorer. The students laughed at his idea.

Ⓓ Students said that there was nowhere left to explore.

_____ ❹ **_"The class looked puzzled."_ In this sentence, the word _puzzled_ means _____**

Ⓐ interested.

Ⓑ confused.

Ⓒ excited.

Ⓓ upset.

_____ ❺ **From whose point of view is the story told?**

Ⓐ John's best friend

Ⓑ Magellan

Ⓒ John

Ⓓ the teacher

_____ ❻ **What changed the class's point of view about being an explorer?**

Ⓐ John convinced the class that being an explorer is fun.

Ⓑ The teacher showed them that a person can explore nearby places.

Ⓒ The teacher admitted that she is an explorer.

Ⓓ The class went on a field trip.

Word Power

Choose the English word from the Vocabulary list that correctly matches the definition.

1 an exciting trip or journey

_____

2 someone who travels to unknown places to find out about them

_____

3 confused

_____

4 something that causes a feeling of great surprise and admiration

_____

Alexander the Great

Reading Tip

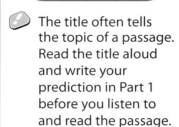 The title often tells the topic of a passage. Read the title aloud and write your prediction in Part 1 before you listen to and read the passage.

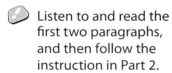 Listen to and read the first two paragraphs, and then follow the instruction in Part 2.

Skill Overview

The topic is the subject of a text. It is the general category to which the ideas of a passage belong. It can often be stated in a word or a phrase. The topic can help readers make predictions about a text.

 26

In 356 B.C., King Philip II and his wife Olympia had a son. They named him Alexander. He was a brave and smart boy who showed strong **leadership**. One famous tale describes a time when Alexander was only 14 years old. King Philip had brought home a horse to add to his **stable**. When Philip tried to **mount** the steed, it bucked and reared. The king was thrown off instantly. He decided that the horse was useless and called for it to be taken away.

Alexander was in the crowd, watching from the sidelines. He insisted that the great horse was being wasted. Many people thought that Alexander's **remarks** were bold because he was only a young boy. But the king challenged Alexander to tame the horse. He promised him that he could keep it if he was successful.

According to legend, the horse instantly calmed when Alexander got close to him. He patted the stallion's neck and spoke softly in his ear. The horse let Alexander lead him. Alexander had noticed that the horse did not like the sight of his great shadow on the ground. Gently, he turned the horse away from its shadow and was able to swing into the saddle without any trouble.

Alexander rode away and back to his father. The crowd cheered this victory, and his father wept in joy. The king gave his son the horse, saying, "My boy, you must find a kingdom big enough for your **ambitions**. Macedonia is too small for you."

The horse was proud and loyal, allowing no one but Alexander to ride him as long as he lived. According to legend, the horse would even lower his body to let Alexander mount him more easily. For years, Alexander rode the **valiant** horse and friend into many battles.

This legend describes some of Alexander's special qualities that allowed him to **conquer** lands and still maintain **respect** as a great leader. He earned the name Alexander the Great.

105

Reading Skill Comprehension Practice

Part 1 Think about what this story will be about. Write your prediction.

Part 2 Think about what will happen in the rest of the passage.

Part 3 If this were a book, predict what the next chapter might be about. Write your prediction below.

Comprehension Review

Fill in the best answer for each question.

❶ This passage is about Alexander the Great. You will probably learn _____

ⓐ where and when Alexander lived.
ⓑ how to make Greek food.
ⓒ where Greece is located.
ⓓ about a new sport.

❷ Which piece of information will probably *not* be in this passage?

ⓐ where Alexander lived
ⓑ something that happened to Alexander
ⓒ how the Greeks built their houses
ⓓ when Alexander was born

❸ Because this is the story of Alexander the Great, it is a _____

ⓐ set of instructions.
ⓑ recipe.
ⓒ letter to the editor.
ⓓ biography.

❹ What caused King Philip to decide his horse was useless?

ⓐ The horse would not move.
ⓑ The horse threw him off.
ⓒ The horse was too small.
ⓓ The horse bit him.

❺ *"When Philip tried to mount the steed, it bucked and reared."*

What does _bucked and reared_ tell you about the horse?

ⓐ It was energetic.
ⓑ It was asleep.
ⓒ It was hungry.
ⓓ It was calm.

❻ Alexander was probably _____

ⓐ lazy.
ⓑ shy.
ⓒ very weak.
ⓓ brave.

Word Power

Choose the English word from the Vocabulary list that correctly matches the definition.

 a strong desire to do or achieve something

_____

 a high opinion; a feeling that someone or something is important

_____

 to win control over someone or something

_____

 very brave

_____

ANCIENT GREECE

Skill Overview

Typeface refers to the size of letters as well as their style, such as italic or boldface print. Different typefaces can be used to organize information and emphasize important words and ideas. Readers can review typeface to help determine the key ideas of a text.

Greece is located on the southern tip of Europe. It borders the Aegean, Ionian, and Mediterranean seas. Greece has a large mainland surrounded by many smaller islands. It is a hot, dry country with mountain ranges.

RELIGION

Ancient Greek life centered on religion. Greeks **worshipped** many gods and goddesses. The Greeks thought that the gods controlled every part of people's lives. Big **decisions** about war and marriage were made only after checking with the gods. Even small decisions were made this way. Poseidon was the god of the seas and rivers. Apollo controlled the Sun and light. Aphrodite was the goddess of love and beauty. Athena was the goddess of war and wisdom.

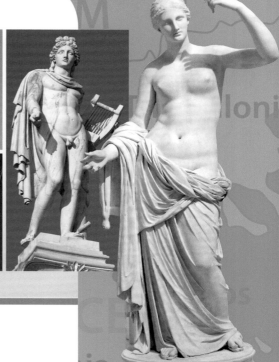

ART AND THEATER

The ancient Greeks made **statues** and beautiful temples for the gods. Huge wall paintings decorated these buildings. They were called *murals*. The **ruins** of these buildings remain, but the paint wore away long ago. Early Greek plays had religious themes. Later plays began to deal with politics. In 534 B.C., the first public plays were held in Athens. They were performed in open-air theaters shaped like semicircles. Seats were built into the hillsides. Some ancient Greek plays are still performed.

Vocabulary

worship
to have or show a strong feeling of respect and admiration for a god

decision
a choice that is made

statue
an object made from a hard material to look like a person or animal

ruins
the broken parts that are left from an old building or town

astronomy
the study of stars, planets, and space

observe
to watch carefully, especially in order to learn more about it

sanctuary
a sacred or holy place

treatment
something done to cure an illness or care for a sick person

SCIENCE AND MEDICINE

The ancient Greeks were interested in science. They made advances in biology, mathematics, **astronomy**, and geography. They based what they knew on what they **observed** in the world. They were the first people in Europe to do this.

An important area of science for the Greeks was medicine. Long ago, the Greeks thought that illness was a punishment from the gods. **Sanctuaries** were built all over Greece. These were holy places to honor the god of medicine. People would spend the night at a sanctuary and pray for a cure. Later, the Greeks came up with **treatments** for diseases. A Greek doctor named Hippocrates came up with many of these treatments. He is called the Father of Modern Medicine.

Reading Skill Comprehension Practice

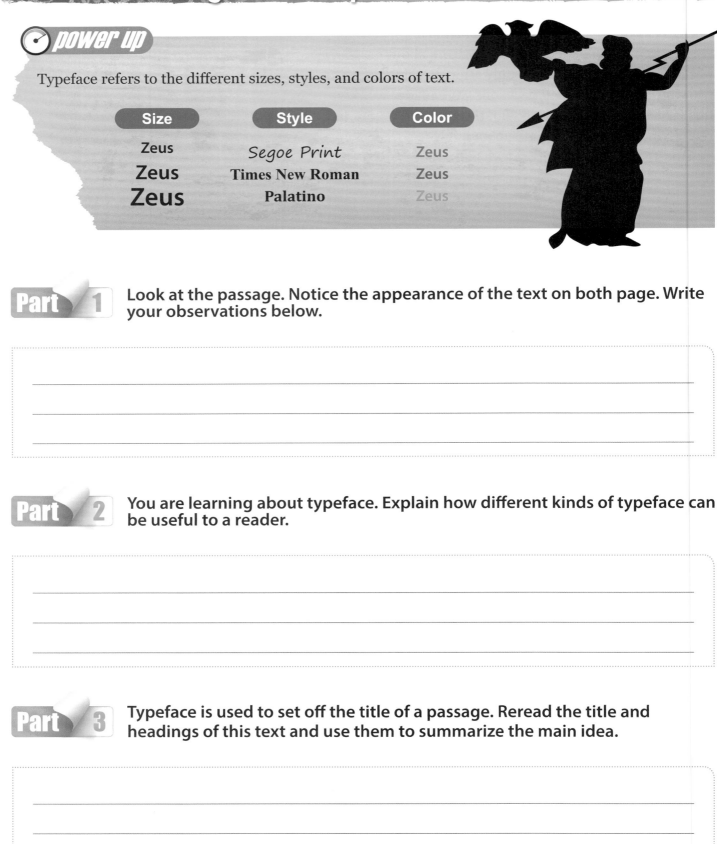

power up

Typeface refers to the different sizes, styles, and colors of text.

Size	Style	Color
Zeus	*Segoe Print*	Zeus
Zeus	**Times New Roman**	Zeus
Zeus	Palatino	Zeus

Part 1 Look at the passage. Notice the appearance of the text on both page. Write your observations below.

_____

_____

_____

Part 2 You are learning about typeface. Explain how different kinds of typeface can be useful to a reader.

_____

_____

_____

Part 3 Typeface is used to set off the title of a passage. Reread the title and headings of this text and use them to summarize the main idea.

_____

_____

_____

Comprehension Review

Fill in the best answer for each question.

_____ ❶ The typeface tells you that _____ is an important topic in this passage.
Ⓐ life in a Greek home
Ⓑ Greek food
Ⓒ Greek theater and art
Ⓓ Greek rivers

_____ ❷ Which one is *not* an important topic in this passage?
Ⓐ Greek religion
Ⓑ Greek public plays
Ⓒ Greek science
Ⓓ Greek art

_____ ❸ Why is Religion in large typeface?
Ⓐ It is the first topic.
Ⓑ It is not very important.
Ⓒ It comes before a paragraph.
Ⓓ It is an important topic.

_____ ❹ You would probably *not* see _____ if you visited Greece.
Ⓐ an icecap
Ⓑ the Adriatic Sea
Ⓒ a mountain
Ⓓ an island

_____ ❺ Why did the Greeks check with the gods before making most decisions?
Ⓐ Greek law said that they had to check with the gods.
Ⓑ They did not have enough information to make decisions.
Ⓒ They thought the gods controlled every part of people's lives.
Ⓓ Most Greeks did not believe the gods were important.

_____ ❻ If the Greeks wanted to win a big battle, they would probably check with _____ before fighting.
Ⓐ Poseidon
Ⓑ Athena
Ⓒ Apollo
Ⓓ Hippocrates

Word Power

Choose the English word from the Vocabulary list that correctly matches the definition.

 the study of stars, planets, and space

_____

 a choice that is made

_____

 a sacred or holy place

_____

 the broken parts that are left from an old building or town

_____

SCHOOL GARBAGE

Skill Overview

A proposition-and-support pattern is a text structure in which a problem or an idea is presented and then one or more solutions are proposed. Proposition-and-support writing contains common words that can help readers recognize the pattern.

There is too much garbage at our school. Have you ever noticed how full the trash cans are at the end of the day? If you looked through the trash cans, you would find plastic, **foam**, glass bottles, food waste, paper, and much more. Many of these items can be recycled, or we could **avoid** their use altogether.

One solution to the problem is to set up a **recycling program** at our school. Next to the trash cans, we could have recycling bins for paper, cans, and plastic. In every classroom, there could be a recycling bin for paper. Students could be in charge of running the recycling program once it is in place.

Another solution is for students and teachers to think about how they **pack** their lunches. Instead of paper lunch bags, we could bring **reusable** cloth bags or tin lunch boxes. We could use reusable plastic **containers** instead of plastic bags. We could bring cloth napkins instead of paper ones. We could also bring real **silverware** instead of plastic. And how about all the juice boxes and soda cans we bring? Instead, we could use a reusable sports bottle for our drinks.

If both of these ideas were put in place, we would have a lot less garbage at our school.

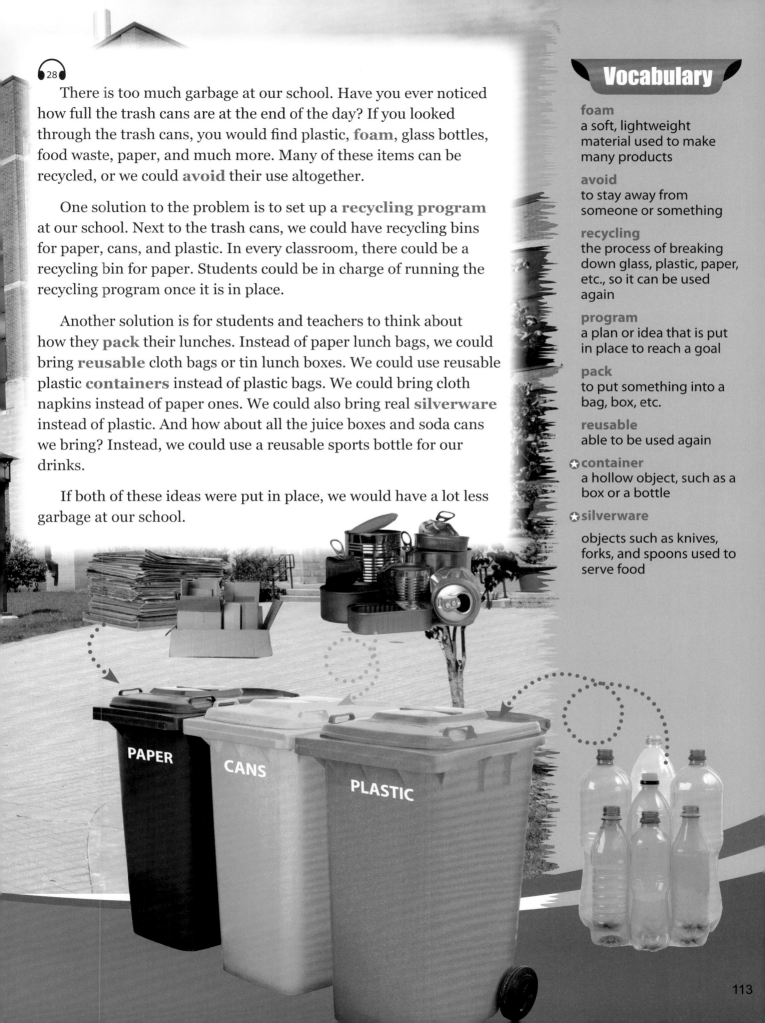

Vocabulary

foam
a soft, lightweight material used to make many products

avoid
to stay away from someone or something

recycling
the process of breaking down glass, plastic, paper, etc., so it can be used again

program
a plan or idea that is put in place to reach a goal

pack
to put something into a bag, box, etc.

reusable
able to be used again

☆**container**
a hollow object, such as a box or a bottle

☆**silverware**
objects such as knives, forks, and spoons used to serve food

PAPER

CANS

PLASTIC

Reading Skill Comprehension Practice

Part 1 Describe the problem addressed in this passage.

 _____

Part 2 Write the two proposed solutions to the problem.

 1. _____

 2. _____

Part 3 Write three key words from the passage tell you it is a proposition-and-support text.

- _____   - _____   - _____

Comprehension Review

Fill in the best answer for each question.

_____ **1** *"There is too much garbage at our school."* **Which sentence supports this claim?**
Ⓐ Bring a reusable cloth bag or a tin lunch box.
Ⓑ We could also bring real silverware.
Ⓒ Many of these items can be recycled.
Ⓓ Have you ever noticed how full the trash cans are?

_____ **2** **Which sentence offers a solution to the problem of too much garbage?**
Ⓐ The trash cans are too full.
Ⓑ And how about all the juice boxes and soda cans we bring?
Ⓒ There is too much garbage at our school.
Ⓓ Next to the trash cans, we could have recycling bins.

_____ **3** *"And how about all the juice boxes and soda cans we bring?"* **Which sentence offers a solution to this problem?**
Ⓐ In every classroom, there could be a recycling bin for paper.
Ⓑ We could bring a reusable cloth bag or a tin lunch box.
Ⓒ Instead, we could use reusable sports bottles for our drinks.
Ⓓ We could bring cloth napkins instead of paper ones.

_____ **4** *"Students could be in charge of running the recycling program once it is in place."* **In this sentence, what does _once it is in place_ mean?**
Ⓐ after the program has been set up
Ⓑ after the program sat down
Ⓒ after the program stopped
Ⓓ after the program has a location

_____ **5** **The author would probably agree that _____**
Ⓐ reusable bags are a good idea.
Ⓑ people should bring more soda cans to school.
Ⓒ it doesn't matter how much you throw away.
Ⓓ everyone can help reduce the amount of garbage at school.

_____ **6** **What is the author's purpose?**
Ⓐ to get you to buy something
Ⓑ to persuade you to do something
Ⓒ to inform you about something
Ⓓ to share a personal experience

Word Power

Choose the English word from the Vocabulary list that correctly matches the definition.

1 the process of breaking down glass, plastic, paper, etc., so it can be used again
_____

2 able to be used again
_____

3 a plan or idea that is put in place in order to reach a goal
_____

4 to stay away from someone or something
_____

LESSON 29
Summarizing

Mission Control Center

Reading Tip

One way to begin summarizing a text is to note important vocabulary words found within the passage.

Another good strategy is to summarize a text in writing.

Houston, Texas

Johnson Space Center

Skill Overview

A summary is a few sentences that tell the main idea of a passage. Summarizing requires readers to eliminate unnecessary information, categorize details, generalize information, and use concise language. Summarizing helps with recall and comprehension.

UPI PHOTO / NASA / NEWSCOM

116

A shuttle astronaut training in the Neutral Buoyancy Laboratory.

Astronauts in training

The United States is one of the leading countries for training **astronauts**. Astronauts in the United States begin their training at the Johnson Space Center in Houston, Texas. The center was first opened in 1961.

The Johnson Space Center has a famous room called the Mission Control Center. This is where people on Earth **direct** the space missions and talk to astronauts in space. They help the astronauts with the work they are doing. The Mission Control Center also watches over the astronauts and their **spacecrafts** to be sure they are safe.

The Johnson Space Center was named in honor of **former** president Lyndon B. Johnson, a Texas native. He was president in the 1960s during a worldwide push to **land** people on the moon for the first time.

What do astronauts do at the Johnson Space Center? They spend a lot of time in class, just as you do in school. They must learn the many **skills** they will need during their space travels.

Astronauts travel into space in groups. So, they **train** with people they will work with in space. It is very important that astronauts work together as a team. Every person has a job to do. They succeed or fail together, just as any team does.

Astronauts also have to work with people on Earth who help them during their trips into space. These people work in the Mission Control Center. There is a lot of **teamwork** needed in space travel!

Vocabulary

astronaut
a person who travels into space

direct
to control the operations of

spacecraft
a vehicle used for travel in space

former
previous; occurring in the past

land
to put someone or something on the ground after a flight

skill
the ability to do something well

train
to prepare by practicing

★ **teamwork**
the combined action of a group

Reading Skill Comprehension Practice

Part 1 Choose 10 important words from the passage and write them below.

☑ _____ ☑ _____ ☑ _____ ☑ _____ ☑ _____

☑ _____ ☑ _____ ☑ _____ ☑ _____ ☑ _____

Part 2 Fill in the graphic organizer below with the main idea of the passage and key ideas from the paragraphs.

Key Idea
_____
_____

Key Idea
_____
_____

Main Idea
_____
_____

Key Idea
_____
_____

Key Idea
_____
_____

Part 3 Underline the main topic in the passage and put a star next to it. Then underline the key ideas and number them in the order you think makes the most sense. Write them down here.

★ _____

1. _____

2. _____

3. _____

4. _____

Comprehension Review

Fill in the best answer for each question.

_____ **①** **Which sentence *best* summarizes the second paragraph of the passage?**

Ⓐ What do astronauts do at the Johnson Space Center?

Ⓑ The Johnson Space Center has a famous Mission Control Center.

Ⓒ The Mission Control Center has people who talk to astronauts and help them with their work.

Ⓓ Astronauts work with the team at the Mission Control Center.

_____ **②** **Which sentence is a good summary of what astronauts do at the Johnson Space Center?**

Ⓐ They go to class, train with a team, and work with the people at the Mission Control Center.

Ⓑ They go to class.

Ⓒ They train with the people they will work with in space.

Ⓓ They work with the Mission Control Center team.

_____ **③** **Which sentence *best* explains how the Johnson Space Center got its name?**

Ⓐ It is named for President Johnson, who was from Texas.

Ⓑ It is named for President Lyndon Johnson, who was president during the 1960s, when there was a push to land people on the moon.

Ⓒ It got its name from a president who wanted to go to the moon.

Ⓓ It got its name from its location: Houston, Texas.

_____ **④** **Why do you think the Johnson Space Center is located in Texas?**

Ⓐ Other states did not want to have a space center.

Ⓑ The climate of Texas is best for space travel.

Ⓒ There was a worldwide push during the 1960s to land a person on the moon.

Ⓓ President Lyndon B. Johnson was from Texas.

_____ **⑤** **What is the purpose of this passage?**

Ⓐ to inform

Ⓑ to give an opinion

Ⓒ to persuade

Ⓓ to tell a personal story

_____ **⑥** **Which activity is *not* performed by astronauts at the Johnson Space Center?**

Ⓐ going to class

Ⓑ training with a team

Ⓒ watching over astronauts and spacecraft

Ⓓ working with the team at the Mission Control Center

Word Power

Choose the English word from the Vocabulary list that correctly matches the definition.

 to control the operations of

_____

 to prepare by practicing

_____

 previous; occurring in the past

 a person who travels into space

Skill Overview

Questioning is an important skill that keeps readers actively engaged. This strategy helps them understand what has been read and promotes critical thinking. Questions can be asked before, during, and after reading.

Reading Tip

- Based on the title, what questions do you have before reading this passage? Write your questions down in the first column of Part 1 before you listen to and read the passage.

- One type of question is the general **thought-provoking query**; another type is the more specific, **clarifying question**. Both types are valuable, but they yield different information.

An Energetic World

🎧 30

   Do you know what makes the clouds move across the sky? Do you know how they formed there in the first place? Something makes the trees grow taller. The birds use something all day long to help them fly, feed, and stay safe from predators. That something is energy. Even the car you drove to the park needed energy to get there.

Energy from the Sun

Believe it or not, almost all the energy used at the park came from the Sun. The Sun is a **giant** ball of hot gases with a lot of energy. That energy is sent to Earth through heat and light **radiation**. The Sun creates so much energy that it is always shooting out **photons**. Photons are tiny packets of energy. They travel quickly through space until they arrive at Earth.

Some photons hit air **molecules** in the atmosphere. Then those air molecules become warmer. The air on the side of the planet facing the sun heats up more than the side facing away. Hot air **expands** and cold air **contracts**. So, the hot air spreads out to where the cold air is shrinking. When this happens, winds are created.

Photons also hit water molecules in the oceans and other water bodies. These molecules become warmer, too. Some of them heat so much that they become gaseous and evaporate. Because they are warm, they rise into the atmosphere. Soon after, they arrive at the top, where the air is colder. There, they **condense** into water vapor and become clouds.

Other photons hit **chlorophyll** molecules stored in tree leaves. Those molecules grab the energy in the photons. They use the energy to nourish the tree by making food. The tree uses that food to grow and produce new seeds and fruit. Some of the photons hit the birds, but the birds don't use those photons much. Instead, they eat the energy-filled seeds and fruit from the trees and other plants, which were energized by the photons. The birds use the energy from their food to fly, grow, and reproduce.

When dinosaurs lived, the plants used photons from the sun to store energy. When the plants died and got buried underground, the energy remained in the plants. These plants were squeezed and compressed over millions of years. In time, the plants turned into oil. The oil was then converted into gasoline and pumped into your car.

Vocabulary

giant
extremely large

radiation
energy from heat or light that cannot be seen

⭐**photon**
the basic unit of electromagnetic radiation, or energy

molecule
the smallest part of a substance that cannot be divided without changing form

expand
to increase in size, number, or importance

contract
to make or become shorter, narrower or generally smaller

condense
to change or make something change from a gas to a liquid or solid state

⭐**chlorophyll**
the green pigment, or color, found in the chloroplasts of plants

Reading Skill Comprehension Practice

Questions BEFORE reading	Questions DURING reading	Questions AFTER reading
→ attempt to <u>predict</u> what the story is about	→ concern <u>clarifications</u> about the text	→ clarify ideas about the topic that the text does not address

Part 1 Fill in the chart below.

Questions I Have BEFORE Reading	Questions I Have DURING Reading	Questions I Have AFTER Reading
1. What does "an energetic world" mean?	**1.** How does energy make all those things in the first paragraph happen?	**1.** How is oil converted into gasoline?
2.	**2.**	**2.**
3.	**3.**	**3.**

Part 2 Write one of each type of question below.

General Question: _____

Specific Question: _____

Comprehension Review

Fill in the best answer for each question.

_____ **1** *"What is a photon?"*

Which sentence answers this question?

ⓐ The sun is a giant ball of hot gases with a lot of energy.

ⓑ Some of them heat so much that they become gaseous and evaporate.

ⓒ Photons are tiny packets of energy.

ⓓ Photons travel quickly through space.

_____ **2** **Which question is *not* answered in this passage?**

ⓐ How are winds created?

ⓑ What do birds do with the energy they get from their food?

ⓒ How do photons get to Earth?

ⓓ How did dinosaurs use energy?

_____ **3** *"The photons travel quickly through space until they arrive at Earth."*

Which question does this answer?

ⓐ How big are photons?

ⓑ How does the Sun's energy get to Earth?

ⓒ How does the Sun get energy?

ⓓ How do clouds move?

_____ **4** **Unlike hot air, cold air _____**

ⓐ contracts.

ⓑ helps to form winds.

ⓒ is made of air molecules.

ⓓ can be found on Earth.

_____ **5** **The *main* purpose of the passage is to _____**

ⓐ get you to use less gas.

ⓑ explain how photons travel through space.

ⓒ convince you to help save the planet.

ⓓ show how all things are connected through energy.

_____ **6** **Why do trees need chlorophyll?**

ⓐ Chlorophyll turns plants into oil.

ⓑ Chlorophyll attracts birds, which eat trees' seeds.

ⓒ Chlorophyll captures energy and produces food.

ⓓ Chlorophyll creates leaves.

Word Power

Choose the English word from the Vocabulary list that correctly matches the definition.

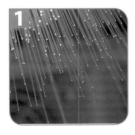 **1** the basic unit of electromagnetic radiation, or energy

_____

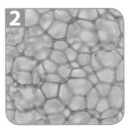 **2** the green pigment, or color, found in the chloroplasts of plants

_____

 **3** the smallest part of a substance that cannot be divided without changing form

_____

 **4** energy from heat or light that cannot be seen

_____

Review Test

Questions 1–10: Read the passage, look at the map, and answer the questions. Fill in the answer choice you think is correct.

A Southeastern State: Florida

Florida's nickname is the Sunshine State. So it's no surprise that the climate there is warm and sunny. The main reason for its balmy weather? Florida is the southernmost state in the continental United States. Year-round warm weather is why many people come to Florida. About 69 million tourists visit Florida's theme parks, resorts, and beaches each year. Because much of Florida is a peninsula, it has plenty of beaches. Florida's coastline is 1,350 miles long—only Alaska's is longer.

Florida's warm weather especially attracts elderly people. About 30 percent of Floridians are more than 55 years old.

Because Florida is so close to Latin America, it is known as the Gateway of the Americas. Florida draws many immigrants from the Caribbean, especially Haiti and Jamaica. Others come from Central and South American nations, such as Nicaragua and Colombia. About 17 percent of Floridians are Latin Americans.

The island-nation of Cuba is only 100 miles from Florida. Because of its closeness, Cubans make up one-third of Floridians born outside the United States. About one-quarter of the population of Miami is Cuban.

Florida lies at the southeastern edge of the United States.

Growing Fast

Florida is a fast-growing state with a strong economy. The banking business and the computer and electronic equipment industries bring in a lot of money. Another big industry is tourism. A large number of Floridians work in hotels, theme parks, and restaurants.

Like many southern states, the warm climate of Florida is good for growing food. Florida is a center for citrus growing. The state produces four-fifths of all orange and grapefruit products in the United States. It is second only to California in growing vegetables.

Florida's weather isn't always pleasant. The state is in the path of hurricanes. They often strike during summer and fall and cause much damage. Still, Floridians have become used to these storms. For them, the good of living in Florida outweighs the bad.

1 Which sentence tells the main idea of the third paragraph? *Lesson 4*

  Ⓐ Florida's location is the reason for its warm and sunny climate.

  Ⓑ About 17 percent of Floridians are Latin Americans.

  Ⓒ Florida draws many immigrants from Latin America because of its location.

  Ⓓ Florida has a fast-growing economy.

2 Why is Florida's climate warm and sunny much of the year? *Lesson 23*

  Ⓐ About 69 million tourists visit Florida's theme parks, resorts, and beaches each year.

  Ⓑ Florida is the southernmost state in the continental United States.

  Ⓒ The state is in the path of hurricanes.

  Ⓓ Florida's coastline is 1,350 miles long.

3 Which question helps you remember information about Florida's climate? *Lesson 30*

  Ⓐ How many tourists come to Florida each year?

  Ⓑ What crops are grown in Florida?

  Ⓒ Where do most people in Florida live?

  Ⓓ Why is Florida's weather warm and sunny most of the time?

4 The typeface tells you that _____ is an important phrase. *Lesson 27*

  Ⓐ Growing Fast

  Ⓑ a large number

  Ⓒ warm weather

  Ⓓ these storms

5 This article can help you _____ *Lesson 22*

  Ⓐ find a hotel in Florida.

  Ⓑ get money for a class trip to Florida.

  Ⓒ learn about Florida.

  Ⓓ get directions to Florida.

6 *"A Southeastern State: Florida"*
This title tells you that this passage will probably be about _____ *Lesson 18*

  Ⓐ ocean life.

  Ⓑ every southeast state.

  Ⓒ staying safe.

  Ⓓ Florida.

7 How is Florida like other southern U.S. states? *Lesson 5*

  Ⓐ It produces four-fifths of all orange and grapefruit products.

  Ⓑ Florida is a fast-growing state.

  Ⓒ It has a warm climate that is good for growing food.

  Ⓓ Cuba is only 100 miles from Florida.

8 What does the caption tell you? *Lesson 13*

  Ⓐ where Cuba is located

  Ⓑ where Florida is located

  Ⓒ where the United States is located

  Ⓓ why people like to visit Florida

9 Which two bodies of water surround Florida? *Lesson 14*

  Ⓐ the Atlantic Ocean and the Gulf of Mexico

  Ⓑ Naples and Miami

  Ⓒ the Atlantic Ocean and Cuba

  Ⓓ Haiti and Jamaica

10 If you did not remember how many tourists visit Florida, you could _____ *Lesson 11*

  Ⓐ read the title.

  Ⓑ read the first paragraph again.

  Ⓒ study the map.

  Ⓓ draw a picture.

Eddie Gomez

Dear Jerry,

I'm writing to apologize to you for what happened yesterday. I didn't get a chance to tell you the whole story. So I will now. First of all, I only meant to borrow your bicycle for about 15 minutes. The thing is, I wanted to go to Sound Town to buy a new CD. My mom couldn't take me, and my bike is broken. I was pretty desperate when I saw your bike on your front lawn. I didn't see you around, and the only reason I didn't ring your doorbell was that I didn't want to bother anybody, in case they were sleeping or watching TV or something. Also, I didn't think you'd miss the bike for such a short time. And I guess I thought that somehow if you did notice it was gone, you'd know I took it. I don't know why I thought that.

I guess I should have left a note, but I didn't have any paper handy. Anyway, I was going to bring your bike back as soon as I bought the CD. The problem was, I ran into Jimmy, Angel, and a few of the guys in Sound Town. They wanted to bike over to the mall. I shouldn't have gone with them, but they wanted to get a slice of pizza, and I was hungry.

When the police stopped me at the mall, I was shocked. They said I had stolen your bike. They took the bike and put me in the police car. I told them I only borrowed the bike, but they didn't listen. They just said they were going to arrest me and tell my parents. I was really upset and scared. That's why when they drove me to your house to make sure it was your bike, I freaked out. I yelled at you for calling the police. That was totally wrong. I should have apologized to you right then. Why wouldn't you think someone had stolen your bike? I mean, you had no way of knowing I had borrowed it.

I acted even worse after you and your mom told the police to let me go. I should have thanked you for keeping me out of trouble. But I guess I was too weirded out by what had happened.

Now I realize I was to blame right from the start. I should have asked you first if I could borrow the bike. I had no right to take it (even though I meant to return it — honest). Anyway, I'm really sorry. I hope you will forgive me for the dumb thing I did.

Your friend,

Eddie

11 Which of these is **not** a reason Eddie took Jerry's bike without asking? *Lesson 28*

- (A) Eddie was angry at Jerry.
- (B) Eddie's mom couldn't take him.
- (C) Eddie's bike was broken.
- (D) Eddie didn't want to bother anybody by ringing the doorbell.

12 Because this is a letter, it will probably _____ *Lesson 16*

- (A) have headings and titles.
- (B) be written from one person to another.
- (C) have study questions at the end.
- (D) tell you how to do something.

13 Why did Eddie write this letter? *Lesson 17*

- (A) to apologize for taking Jerry's bike
- (B) to ask if he could borrow Jerry's bike
- (C) to ask if he could borrow money to go to Sound Town
- (D) to ask Jerry where to buy a good bike

14 Which sentence is an opinion? *Lesson 20*

- (A) I didn't have any paper handy.
- (B) I ran into Jimmy, Angel, and a few of the guys in Sound Town.
- (C) They took the bike and put me in the police car.
- (D) I acted even worse after you and your mom told the police to let me go.

15 Eddie was put in the police car **after** _____ *Lesson 19*

- (A) Jerry and his mom told the police to let Eddie go.
- (B) he wrote the letter to Jerry.
- (C) he took Jerry's bike.
- (D) Jerry got his bike back.

16 *"Dear Jerry,"*
This helps you predict that you will read _____ *Lesson 21*

- (A) an encyclopedia.
- (B) a map.
- (C) a letter.
- (D) a newspaper article.

17 You already know how it feels to make a mistake. This helps you understand _____ *Lesson 9*

- (A) what Sound Town is.
- (B) what Jerry's bike looked like.
- (C) how to write a letter.
- (D) why Eddie wrote an apology letter.

18 *"I'm writing to apologize to you for what happened yesterday."*
This topic sentence tells you that Eddie _____ *Lesson 8*

- (A) will ask Jerry for money.
- (B) will tell Jerry how to get to Eddie's house.
- (C) will tell Jerry that Eddie is sorry for something.
- (D) will be invited to a party.

Questions 19–24: Read the passage and then answer the questions on the following page. Fill in the answer choice you think is correct.

The Golden Touch

Once there was a king named Midas who lived in an area that we now call Turkey. Midas was not a bad man, but he was very greedy.

One day a man named Silenus got lost in Midas's kingdom. Midas believed in helping travelers, so he offered to help Silenus return home. Silenus told Midas that he lived with the god Dionysus (dy-u-NY-suhs). Midas arranged to have the man taken home, and soon after, Dionysus appeared before the king.

"I would like to give you a reward for helping my friend," Dionysus said. "Ask me for anything and, if I can, I will grant your wish." Midas knew he had only one wish, so he wanted to be very careful about his choice.

"I would like everything I touch to turn to gold," Midas said. Dionysus looked at the king. "Are you certain that is what you desire?" he asked.

"Yes," Midas answered. "I am positive."

Dionysus granted the king's wish. Midas was excited to immediately put the wish to the test. He touched a twig and a stone—they turned to solid gold. "I got my wish!" exclaimed the king. "Now I will be the richest man in the world!" Midas ran into his palace and touched everything from floor to ceiling. Before he knew it, half the day had gone by and he realized how hungry he was. He went into his dining hall and sat at his golden table.

Midas commanded his servants to bring him food, and they obeyed. Hungrily, Midas grabbed a loaf of bread from the golden plate. As soon as he did, it turned to gold. He took an apple in his hand, but the same thing happened. Midas told his servants to feed him, but as soon as the food touched his lips, it became hard, cold metal. Now he realized his mistake.

"Dionysus!" he cried. "What will I do? I will starve to death because of my wish!"

Dionysus heard Midas and took pity on him. "Not far from your palace is the River Pactolus," he told the king. "Go there and wash yourself in it. Your golden touch will be washed away."

19 What caused King Midas to fear that he would starve?   Lesson 2

- (A) His food turned to gold, so he could not eat it.
- (B) Dionysus would not give him food.
- (C) His servants were angry at him and would not bring him food.
- (D) There was no food in the kingdom.

20 Which of these describes King Midas?   Lesson 7

- (A) jealous and mean
- (B) shy and quiet
- (C) kind but greedy
- (D) friendly but dishonest

21 What was the **first** thing King Midas did after Dionysus granted his wish?   Lesson 10

- (A) He bathed in the river.
- (B) He asked his servants to bring him food.
- (C) He asked Dionysus to take away his wish.
- (D) He turned a twig and a stone to gold.

22 What problem did the golden touch cause for King Midas?   Lesson 12

- (A) Everyone became jealous of him.
- (B) His food turned to gold, so he could not eat.
- (C) Dionysus grew angry at him.
- (D) He realized he was bored with gold.

23 Which is a good way to tell someone about King Midas?   Lesson 25

- (A) King Midas was greedy, so when he got a wish, he wished to change everything to gold. When his wish came true, he found out that the golden touch changed all his food to gold, so he could not eat. He washed himself in the river, and his golden touch went away.
- (B) King Midas helped Silenus return home. Then he got a reward. He wanted to change everything to gold, and he did.
- (C) King Midas lived in what is now Turkey. He helped a man return home, and then he changed everything to gold. The river still has gold dust in it.
- (D) King Midas was a greedy man, so Dionysus gave him a wish. Midas wished to turn everything to gold. Then he asked his servants for food and they brought it to him.

24 People who enjoy reading about _____ would like this story.   Lesson 6

- (A) famous astronauts
- (B) math brain teasers
- (C) myths and legends
- (D) sports

Read the time line and then answer the questions. Fill in the answer choice you think is correct.

Martin Luther King Jr.

Important Dates

1929: Born in Atlanta, Georgia

1948: Became a Baptist minister

1957: Formed the Southern Christian Leadership Conference to fight segregation and gain civil rights for African Americans

1962: Went to jail for protesting segregation in Birmingham, Alabama

1963: Helped organize the March on Washington, D.C. Delivers his "I Have a Dream" speech

1964: Awarded the Nobel Peace Prize

1967: Organized the Poor People's Campaign to get jobs for poor people

1968: Assassinated in Memphis, Tennessee

25 Which one happened **first**?   Lesson 15

(A) Martin Luther King Jr. went to jail for protesting segregation.

(B) Martin Luther King Jr. was awarded the Nobel Peace Prize.

(C) Martin Luther King Jr. became a Baptist minister.

(D) Martin Luther King Jr. was assassinated in Memphis, Tennessee.

26 This passage is about Martin Luther King Jr. You can predict that the time line is about _____   Lesson 26

(A) settling the American West.

(B) the American Revolution.

(C) Martin Luther King Jr.'s life.

(D) the Civil War.

27 The title tells you that this is about _____
Lesson 1

(A) the life of Martin Luther King Jr.

(B) life in the American West.

(C) how to make something.

(D) the American Indians.

28 The heading tells you that this is a _____
Lesson 3

(A) list of new words.

(B) time line of important dates.

(C) set of instructions.

(D) list of names to remember.

29 Which sentence tells you the most important idea?   Lesson 24

   (A) Martin Luther King Jr. was a Baptist minister.

   (B) He also wanted the government to help poor Americans of all colors.

   (C) The reason was to demand equal justice for African Americans.

   (D) He led the civil rights movement from the mid-1950s until his assassination in 1968.

30 Which of these would be a good title for the time line?   Lesson 29

   (A) Important Events of the 1960s

   (B) Settling the Colonies

   (C) Martin Luther King Jr.'s Fight for Civil Rights

   (D) African Americans: From Slavery to Freedom

Answers

1-5	6-10	11-15	16-20	21-25	26-30
CBDAC	DCBAB	ABADC	CDCAC	ABACC	DBACC

131